Secrets

Still waters run deep between old friends ...

Wongan Creek Series
Book 2

Juanita Kees

Published by Juanita Kees (Kees2Create)

eBook ISBN: 9780645631999

Paperback ISBN: 9781763632400

Cover Design Copyright © by Paradox Book Cover Designs & Formatting

Secrets

Juanita Kees

Still waters run deep between old friends …

Harley Baker stands to lose everything when spray drift from his neighbour's toxic herbicides destroys his crop. But arguments are tricky when it comes to Tameka Chalmers. Financial ruin is only a small part of the nightmare that keeps him away from the woman he's always loved.

Tameka Chalmers knows that her father's farming methods are outdated, inefficient, and even dangerous. There's so much she would like to do differently, but her father's rule is absolute, and she must do as she's told or be prepared for the consequences.

When Harley confronts her about the damage to his crop, the interaction triggers an unexpected chain reaction that throws everything she's ever known into question. As long buried secrets rise to the surface, everything they believed to be true will be challenged. Can they rise from the ashes of lies and betrayal when each step they take brings danger closer to their door?

About the Author

Finding hope in country towns with dark secrets ...

Juanita escapes the real world to create emotionally engaging stories steeped in crime, suspense, mystery, and intrigue. Her books are set in dusty, rural outback Australia and on the NASCAR racetracks of America. Her small-town USA and Australian rural stories have made the Amazon bestseller and top 100 lists. Juanita also likes to dabble in the ponds of fantasy and paranormal with Greek gods brought to life in the 21st century.

Juanita graduated college with distinctions and a diploma in Proofreading, Editing and Publishing in 2011 and started her freelance writing business, Kees2Create Words. As a developmental and structural editor, she assists writers to polish their manuscripts for submission. In 2012, she achieved her dream of becoming a published author and now has multiple novels on the market.

When she's not working, writing, editing, or proofreading, Juanita enjoys travelling to discover new worlds for inspiration. Mother to two handsome heroes and partner to a car enthusiast, Juanita also has a passion for fast cars and country living.

Juanita loves to talk books with readers and would love to connect. Contact her via:

Amazon Author:
https://www.amazon.com/author/juanitakees
Website:
https://juanitakees.com/contact/
Kees2Create Words Editing:
https://kees2createwords.com/
BookBub:
https://www.bookbub.com/authors/juanita-kees
Newsletter:
https://kees2createwords.substack.com/embed
Goodreads:
https://www.goodreads.com/author/show/6454477.
Juanita_Kees
Book Love Book Club:
https://www.facebook.com/groups/
607880523038543

*For those who will never truly be able to answer the
question everyone will ask — why did you stay?*

Chapter One

Tameka confiscated the rope Harley's dog had destroyed along with three hundred square metres of her newly sown barley field.

'Hooley Dooley, Loki, what have you done?'

Oh, Harley Baker would pay for this, for sure. She paid no attention to Loki's attempts to claim her attention even though twenty-three kilograms of Catahoula Leopard dog leaping at her torso wasn't easy to ignore.

'Sit down!' Tameka said sternly, surprised when Loki obeyed and looked at her with his melt-your-heart eyes. No-one melted her heart. Not Harley Baker and not his dog either. 'Bad dog.'

Loki gave a short bark and offered up a reconciliatory doggy grin.

'Don't smile at me.'

She looked over the dog's head at the destruction in his wake and ignored the paw that scratched at the leg of her denims in a bid for attention.

Her neatly ploughed and planted rows of barley resembled a churned-up dirt bike track after the annual fair in the wake of Loki's destruction, the almost empty container of liquid concentrate mix she'd used for spot-spraying and hadn't had time to put away yet overturned in the soil.

Now there was Loki's health to worry about too. If he'd ingested some of the herbicides her father insisted on using, he could be an extremely sick dog and that would break her heart. No amount of pushing towards using organic herbicides could sway Louis Chalmers away from chemical poisons.

But then no amount of hard work and dedication could make him believe she was worthy of his praise either. No, her dad would be far happier if he'd had a son instead of a daughter.

Loki's adventures in the barley would only prove him right that she was an incompetent farmer and manager who couldn't even keep the gate between the two farms shut — no matter whose fault it was that the dog had chosen her field as his playground.

She set the container upright and checked that the lid was still securely screwed into place as the low gear warble of a four-stroke engine reached her ears. That'd be Harley coming to look for his dog. No four-legged horses for that farm boy. His were all steel-framed, power-hungry two-wheelers as sleek and sexy as he was.

She shivered inside her sheepskin-lined jacket and tugged her beanie down around her ears. A sexy pain in the arse who once had owned her heart.

The 200cc Trojan appeared out of the remains of the morning fog, and Tameka sucked in the cold air, letting it burn down her throat and into her lungs as she watched the bike progress down the firebreak.

When dealing with Harley, she needed a heart of ice, or he'd get under her skin and make her remember what he felt like under his flannel-checked shirt and denims. A distraction she couldn't afford when it made her long for the friendship and love they'd lost.

Oh, she knew exactly what he looked like under those clothes thanks to a dare when they'd been young and stupid. He'd been eighteen and filling out in all the right places when he'd lost his bet about her father letting her manage the farm. She'd made him do two laps of the firebreak around Bakers Hill on his damn bike — naked, wearing only his boots — in the middle of winter. And then there was that one time in his ute … At least he had clothes on today. It would make it much easier to stay angry with him.

He pulled up at the fence, and she let the rhythm of the engine throb through her, itching for a ride. Her father wouldn't have bikes in the field. That's what utes were for. And where the ute didn't go, you walked. She looked at Harley's face under his red beanie. Not only was he wearing clothes, he was also wearing an incredibly angry face. Good, because she was angry too and spoiling for a fight.

'Your bloody dog just wrecked all my hard work. Churned up my field and made it his damn playpen.' Raising her voice over the engine noise, she threw her arms wide across the scene. The culprit sat centre stage for a split second before his brain kicked into gear and he pounded across the field of destruction to greet his owner.

'Sit. Stay,' Harley commanded.

The dog sat his butt in the churned-up soil and peered through the fence, head cocked to one side, ears pinned back and a questioning whine in his voice. Harley cut the engine and pushed down the stand. Denim clung to his thighs as he swung his leg back across the seat.

Tameka tried hard not to appreciate the view while she ignored the hitch of breath in her throat. Watching Harley move had once been her favourite way to spend the day. It still was, except now she did it from the other side of the fence. On the odd occasion they did speak it was as if they were strangers and had never been lovers or even good friends, their conversation polite, stilted and all business.

The easy stride of those long legs, the way he

dragged a hand through his hair when he was annoyed, embarrassed, or simply irritated. His smile and easy laughter, how he used to make her feel — special, wanted, loved — were all happy memories she kept locked in her dreams to chase away the monsters at night.

Today his flannel shirt was red and black, just visible under a black puffer jacket, his footy scarf wrapped around his neck to ward off the morning chill. West Coast Eagles — another reminder of what they'd once had together. Through thick and thin, she'd always be a Dockers fan. Purple would always clash with yellow and blue.

But right this minute it wasn't about the good-natured football rivalry they'd once had between them or the times they'd spent cheering for opposite teams, finding reasons to kiss and make up. That was in the past. Today was all about the partially ruined rows of barley crop she'd have to re-seed.

Harley pushed through the open gate in the fence between their farms. A pang of regret nudged Tameka's heart. She missed the days when he'd come through that gate for reasons that didn't cause a scowl on his face. When they'd been on speaking terms — on kissing terms — except on Derby Day. Back in the years when the competition between her and Harley had been about who could climb the highest in the old gum tree down by the creek or who could sow a row faster.

The only purpose the gate served these days was when Loki nosed it open to chase the birds out of the trees around the dam, or like today, kill and bury his rope for resurrection later.

'I'll come down and weld that bloody gate shut.' He stopped with his boots inches from hers, and she could smell the remnants of his shower soap and toothpaste as he called, 'Loki, heel!'

Loki obeyed, his ice-blue gaze full of apology as he leaned against Harley's leg and begged for an ear scratch.

A pang of regret filled her heart at the way Harley stood so close, his body heat warming her personal space. There'd been a time when she could reach out and tug at his beanie or steal his scarf. Or lean up against him and kiss the spots of colour the cold morning put in his cheeks.

'Might be best.' She raised her eyes from his mouth to his face and caught the grim expression there, her heart sinking at the annoyance in his eyes. 'Who stole your sunshine and rainbows this morning? I'm the one with the churned-up field.'

He whipped off his beanie, shoved it in his jacket pocket and blew out a warm, angry breath that tickled her face.

'That'd be you, Tameka.' He reached inside his puffer jacket, his arm brushing across her chest, and pulled out a cutting with wilted leaves. 'Looks like we're even over Loki's mess because your infernal preference for phenoxies has destroyed almost my entire crop on this side of the fence line.'

Shit. Tameka took the cutting from his hands, stepped back and studied it. Her heart plummeted. Deformed leaves hung limply from the stunted stems; misshapen, brittle, and burnt. Damn it, hadn't she warned her father about spray drift? Harley's towering hops would have copped a good portion of it. With his bines climbing at over ten metres high, there'd be little chance of them avoiding the damage phenoxy spray caused to broadleaf crops. No matter how careful she was about spraying.

Harley shoved a hand through his toffee-coloured hair. 'Long-term, *preventable* herbicide damage. How many times do we need to have this conversation?'

'My hands are tied, Harley.' Anger pushed her heart back up where it belonged. Of course he'd blame her. Everyone would.

'Bullshit. You're the farm manager on Golden Acres. You call the shots.'

And if he believed that, he was dumber than she'd given him credit for. Her father would never let go of the reins completely for as long as he breathed in this life. But Harley wasn't done lashing out at her yet. She would bear the brunt of it — his anger and frustration — knowing he had every right to feel that way, powerless in that there wasn't a damn thing she could do about it, no matter how hard she tried. She stayed silent and let him offload his grievances to the top of her head while she studied the mud.

'Every year I lose crop I can't afford to because you continue to use chemical weed killers. As if the water shortages aren't doing enough damage. Damn it, Tameka, you have no idea the council hoops I have to jump through to get approval to use recycled water until I can get my dam built.'

She shook her head and bit her tongue. As if she hadn't already explored alternatives to phenoxies and tried to convince her dad to use them. And the lack of rain affected her crop as much as it did Harley's, even with their dam as back up.

When she didn't buy into the argument, he continued. 'So, do you know what? Your churned up rows don't quite cut it compared to three hectares of stunted growth that produced little or no damn crop this year.' He closed the gap between them until they stood boot to boot once more.

No, of course they didn't. The back-breaking hours she'd spent on and off the tractor towing the archaic box air seeder with its failing air hoses, tilling the soil, fertilising, checking, measuring, only to have her father inspect it, find it lacking and make her do it all over again — none of it counted. Anger made tears sting her eyes. She fought them back. Tameka Chalmers didn't cry and screw Harley Baker for making her want to.

'Take your dog and your dickatude and get off my land.'

She raised her hands and shoved him hard, catching him off guard so he stumbled back and fell on his arse in the soil. She bent and picked up the tortured remains of Loki's rope and lobbed it at his chest. Then she turned and walked away.

Damn him for invading her space and making her want to spill her guts to him like she used to before. To tell him exactly what she had to do to keep Golden Acres up and running. And the rest. The whole horrible, God damn *miserable* story.

'Tameka, wait.'

She hesitated at Harley's shout but didn't stop or turn around.

'I'm sorry I yelled at you, okay. It's been a bitch of a day, and it's only just bloody started.'

As if every day was freaking paradise for her. He could rot in hell along with his damaged crop. She didn't care what he had to say.

'It's not just the phenoxy damage. Some of the cones on the north-side bines have developed downy mildew. My harvest is down fifty percent thanks to all the damage, and my profit with it. The bank is threatening to foreclose on my loan if I can't make payment. If they won't grant me an extension …'

The desperation in his tone almost had her turning

around, but nothing should make her feel sorry for Harley Baker.

'I'll lose everything.'

Except that. Her heart plummeted to her boots and stopped her in her tracks at the thought of what that meant for Harley and Bakers Hill. She wouldn't wish that kind of ruin on her worst enemy because she knew the cost of it all too well herself.

Chapter Two

Harley watched Tameka's spine stiffen and rubbed at his chest. For such a wispy thing, she still packed a punch. Under that heavy sheepskin jacket, she was whippet-thin with long legs that went all the way up to a tight, fit-in-your-hand arse.

Pity she didn't know how to girl anymore. Not since she'd been ripped from his arms and things had changed between them forever. Regret edged its way into his mind. He missed the girl she used to be. The kind of girl he needed right now. His girl. Simpler times.

She turned and walked back as Loki licked Harley's face then made a play for the rope. He tossed it across the fence, sending the dog chasing back through the gate onto his land.

His arse still in the soil, Harley pulled up his knees,

leaned his elbows on them and hung his head, feeling the tension grip his neck, his heart heavy.

With little crop yield for the market, his loss would be so great he might not be able to hold onto Bakers Hill for much longer. Then he would never see Tameka again, not even from a distance.

Her shadow fell over him in the weak sunshine. 'Well, that sucks.'

He hadn't meant to tell her anything. They didn't talk much these days, not unless it was business-related and totally necessary. He looked up into those almond-shaped, chocolate-brown eyes he'd loved so much, and saw that they too had forgotten how to smile — like her lips. Not that either of them had much to smile about these days.

'I'm in deep shit, Tikki.'

The childhood name slipped from his lips, a reminder of the days when she'd known all his secrets, witnessed all his failures and celebrated his successes. When they'd been friends. Before the Big Bang.

She extended her hand, all long fingers, and short nails and callouses from hard work. He took it and let her pull him back on his feet.

His good mate Tikki had been a tough rival and sworn-to-secrecy confidante growing up, unlike the adult Tameka who'd grown cold and distant. All his fault. But this was business and nothing to do with what they'd once had.

She let go as soon as he was up and shoved her hands into the pockets of her thick jacket. 'When did you hear?'

He dusted the soil from the seat of his denims. 'Last night. I got a call from Greg Saunders to arrange a meeting this week.' As apologetic as the bank manager had been, it hadn't softened the punch of failure, the reality of what he had to face to keep hold of everything he loved. 'I've been up all night going over the figures, trying to scrape something together, some alternative to keep going.'

Tameka pressed her fingers to her temples and closed her eyes, her distress clear in her frown and the downward tug of her mouth. 'What about your mung bean crop? Was that damaged too?'

'No, that's done pretty well. The greenhouses saved the crop from contamination this year, but the cost set me back a bit.' Harley pulled his beanie out of his pocket and tugged it back on. 'It's been an expensive few years. I had no choice but to mortgage the property to have funds to build the dam and the greenhouses. Filling the recycled water tanks we had put in doesn't come cheap either.' Yet another penance to pay for his actions that had caused this whole damn mess.

She opened her eyes to look at him again. 'I'm sorry, Harley. If I could change what happened ...'

But they couldn't. Nothing could stop his father's heart attack from happening or bring Ryan back or change the events of the day he'd lost his best friend. 'Maybe I should take John Bannister up on his offer and sell out.'

'No damn way. That would kill your father, Harley. Bannister will be digging holes all over the land in search of gold and every ounce of sweat your family has put into the soil will be lost. Suck it up, princess, and find a way to deal with the problem that doesn't involve selling out to Wongan Creek Mining.'

Despite his testiness and frustration, he let some of his anger slip away. For a brief moment there he'd caught a glimpse of the old Tikki, the one who delivered tough love and a kick up the butt when he needed it most. It did nothing to help his current situation though, and with gold fever gripping the town, many farmers in the region were jumping to take up the cash offers John Bannister was dealing out. A much easier and cheaper option than to continue to sustain the losses each harvest brought to the region, whatever the cause.

'I've lost a major portion of my hops. The crop will take a year or two at least to recover from the damage this time.'

Time he didn't have when his livelihood relied on every hectare of the bines being profitable and disease-free. He dropped his hands to his hips. Reality kicked like a mule. Having to tell his father that he'd failed would be bad enough, but buckling to the pressure to sell out or have the property repossessed would finish his old man off for sure.

Tameka stepped closer, her hand out to touch his arm. 'I'm sorry. I really am.'

Things might not have been the same between them for a long time, but her apology came from the heart, of that he could be sure. She'd understand the rolling consequences, the casualties both human and financial.

He should stay angry with her and her father. This was all their fault, but he knew better than anyone how stubborn and unpleasant old man Chalmers could be. Tameka would only have followed her father's instructions, and Harley couldn't find it in his heart to lay the blame entirely at her feet. He'd have to man up and face the old bastard himself, no matter how unpleasant it would be. Another hoop to jump through that might be a complete waste of time if he couldn't get the bank to grant him a grace period for repayment.

He hung his head and concentrated on the laces of his steel-capped boots. 'This is a bloody disaster. My four pigs sure as hell won't bring home the bacon.' He grimaced. 'No pun intended.'

In the past that would have drawn a laugh from her, but that beautiful sound he'd missed so much stayed locked in as her lips tightened. Things shouldn't be so awkwardly polite between them. It sucked — almost as much as the water shortage, the dam they no longer shared, and the mess created by her father's insistence on using crop-damaging herbicides.

The installation of greenhouses and recycled water tanks had been an expensive game changer for Bakers Hill and his bank account when Tameka's dad had donned on his double A-sized Arrogant Arsehole boots and decided he no longer wanted to share his water supply with the Bakers. *My land, my dam.* A move that had almost killed Harley's father. The reason he and Mum had to leave the farm and move to town.

And now the damaged crop and the fallout from it when he was the only damn grower and supplier in the southern region of Western Australia — how did you break that kind of news to a man on the edge of another heart attack? How to tell him that the farm their family had worked for four generations might be repossessed unless he could find a way out of this latest disaster.

'So, I have to head into town to tell Dad the bad news. Not the sort of thing I want to talk about over the phone. Damn it, Tikki, it could be years before the crop recovers. Besides the cost, it's not what Dad needs to hear right now.'

Tameka dropped her hand from his arm. 'Look, I know things aren't great between us, but this is my fault, and I should be the one to explain it to your dad. I'll go with you.'

He eyed her warily. It had been a long time since they'd shared a ride in a ute. The last time they had, it hadn't ended well. Nothing like being nailed with your jocks around your ankles bumping uglies with your girl and getting sprung by her dad. Big Bang, no dam, broken friendships, and a lifetime of regret. Young, horny, and stupid.

He'd lost more than his virginity that day. He'd lost his soul mate when she'd shut him out after the huge barney between the families that had followed. They were nineteen, old enough to do the deed. Old enough to carry the consequences. But that was the day her dad had taken her away from him for good.

Could he risk being in the same ute with her again? Almost eight years later when the wounds still bled and he should be angry at her for destroying his crops, yet the mere sight of her sad, beautiful face had his heart dancing a two-step?

'Why would you want to do that?'

Not that he didn't want to ride with her. Oh, hell no. He'd love a second chance to be alone with her, to apologise for the shit he'd caused, to tell her how much he missed her company in spite of all the time apart.

Four out of eight of those years apart he'd spent away at university in Perth doing his bachelor's degree in agriculture and Rural Science. Except for semester breaks when he'd come home to help Dad on the farm. Not enough time at home to heal the rift between them, even if it was possible.

Her dad hadn't let him near her again after the

incident in the ute. And then when Harley had come home for good, it had been to his father's illness, and he'd had to take over the running of the farm and the challenges the fallout with the Chalmers had caused. No time for play or much else.

Could this be the icebreaker, the end to their personal cold war? If he lost Baker's Hill — the last of everything he had — he'd never see her again. And he couldn't walk away from the land without settling a few scores with her father first. Like coming between them the way he had, and almost destroying his family's livelihood.

Tameka shifted on her feet, kicking up a chunk of soil with the toe of her boot. 'It's my spray drift that caused the problem. What if it's affected Travis Bailey's canola crop too? He's got enough on his plate looking after Harry's farm as well as his own. I have to have the facts so I can tell Dad what's going on.'

And that wouldn't be a pleasant conversation. Old man Chalmers wasn't exactly the caring, understanding type. 'Only if you're sure that's what you want to do. I don't want to get you into any trouble.'

She met his gaze, all guts and determination in the set of her chin. 'I have to take responsibility for this and find out the extent of the damage.' Her face softened. 'I really am sorry, Harley. About everything.'

So was he. If he could go back and change the things that had happened in the past … so many things. Like that awful day he'd let his brother go play in the shed on his own, and the day he'd let his dick rule his head and hurt his best friend.

Harley blew out a breath. He couldn't do anything to change the past, and right now the future looked pretty glum too. This could be the last time he spent any time with Tameka. Forever. 'Okay, thanks. I appreciate the backup. It means a lot.'

Because God knows, he needed the support of someone who understood his struggle, and even with the forgotten years between them, Tikki would get the idea of what he was going through. She'd understand why he couldn't fail and let the farm go bankrupt.

She dropped her gaze from his and looked out across the dam. 'No problem.'

'Will you tell your dad where you're going?' Surely after all this time, her dad no longer had the power to stop her from seeing him? They were adults, for God's sake.

'No, he doesn't need to know yet. Not until I have all the facts.'

Harley pressed his fingers to his eyes. An already long day had just grown longer. In the same ute with the girl, he couldn't hold again — that equalled torture — but keeping secrets from Louis Chalmers was a madness he never wanted to revisit. With a man like him, you were damned if you told him the truth and dead meat if he discovered it any other way.

'Keeping secrets is what got us into a load of trouble last time. I won't put you in that position again. Not when we're not friends anymore. I'm not even sure what we are.'

'We're neighbours, Harley, that's all. And what happened between us was a long time ago. This is nothing more than me taking responsibility for my actions. You can drive yourself into town if you bloody want to. I can go alone. Take it or leave it, no skin off my nose.'

And such a pretty nose it was. He'd loved the feel of it nuzzled against his neck. Wanted to feel it there again. Which could never happen, and he had to keep his mind focused on the struggle ahead. 'I'll take it.'

'Great.' The word grated out between her teeth. 'What time do you want to leave?'

'After lunch? Around one-thirty?'

'Pick you up at your gate at one-thirty. If you're not there, I'll know you've changed your mind and gone ahead on your own.'

Loki lurched back through the gate, wriggled between them, and dropped the rope on Harley's boots, tongue hanging out. Harley picked it up and tossed it again, but Loki wasn't buying it. The dog gave a little whine and pawed at his leg.

Harley scratched Loki's ears. 'I'll be there.' Because God help him, he couldn't not be when she was doing the right thing by him.

'And I'll talk to Dad again about looking into alternatives for weed control once I have an idea of the extent of the damage.'

She turned away, but not before he caught the tightening of her lips and the look of resignation on her face. Discussions with Louis Chalmers were never his idea of fun, he didn't figure it would be any different for her. 'Tikki?'

'Don't call me that. We're way past those days now.'

The impact of that statement ricocheted through him as he patted Loki's side. It shouldn't still hurt.

'Did he give you tonnes of shit that day?'

She'd know which day he meant — the one when his heart had died, hers had taken a hammering, and their perfect world that existed only of each other had changed forever.

She cast a quick look over her shoulder and tugged on her lime green beanie. 'You have no idea.'

He wanted to hold her, hug her, but he'd never be that person for her again. 'I'm sorry.' It wasn't anywhere near enough.

Chapter Three

Sorry. That word got tossed around a lot and meant nothing. What the hell was she thinking offering Harley a lift into town? She wasn't his friend — hadn't been for a long time — and if her father found out about it he'd be furious with her.

They didn't even buy their damn supplies in Wongan Creek, never mind attend any community meetings, functions, or events. Dad refused to, ever since he'd cut all ties with the community. Not that he'd bothered to establish many, if any at all.

Tameka made her way between the rows, down the field towards the tractor shed. The acres of rich soil would soon produce bright green sprouts and fill the rolling landscape with a contrast of colour. Like a painting on a canvas.

Damn Harley Baker and his dog for screwing up her

day even more. Damn her heart for pounding from attraction instead of anger. Damn this constant yearning for the togetherness they'd once shared.

She looked past the shed. Down near the creek, the homestead sprawled empty and dying. Dad didn't care about doing maintenance on it. When the door had slammed behind Mum that awful day, he'd stopped caring about anything other than making Tameka's life hell.

Not that it had been much different before that. When a beer or ten and a bottle of whisky changed his personality from zero hero to major arsehole.

You stay away from that Baker boy. If you want to get knocked up and waste your life, get out of my house. If you want to manage this farm, you do as I say and put your back into it, girl.

She hadn't seen her mother leave, hadn't had time to say goodbye or been given the choice to go with her. Instead, she'd been locked in her room to contemplate her sins, forced to stay while her father had delivered his final 'fuck you' to her mother by keeping her there.

Go, Mai! But you fucking go alone, and your daughter stays to pay for being a whore just like her mother.

It was her fault her mum had packed her bags and gone, leaving her dad to manage on his own, and he'd never let her forget it as his mood swings, temper and drinking had grown steadily worse.

Tameka had stayed on the farm hoping her mum would come back for her. Wishing she'd taken her away too the day life changed for the worst at Golden Acres.

Stop snivelling over your mother. She's gone. Never coming back. She didn't fucking want you.

She'd stayed beyond the point of being able to leave her miserable, angry, violently drunk, and emotionally abusive father because she loved the land she worked every day. Because she hoped that things would change. That he'd change. Instead, her father had destroyed everything that signified her mother's presence, burnt it on a bonfire.

His anger had been so tangible that night Tameka had stayed locked in her bedroom and barred the door shut to stop him from smashing his way inside and having another go at her. He'd taken two days to calm down before falling into a drunken sleep, and she'd never seen her mother again.

She pushed away the memory and hitched the seeder to the tractor, feeling the burn in her muscles as the weight dragged at them. She needed to fix the mess Loki had made before her dad found out, and then she had to come up with an excuse as to why she had to make a trip into Wongan Creek because he wouldn't care that his spray drift had destroyed another man's livelihood. He'd see it as a victory.

Two hours later, the ancient box air seeder gave her a reason when the hydraulic air hose lost the will to struggle, burst free from its brass fitting and waved around like a crazed snake under the pressure.

'Bloody hell.' Tameka scrambled to shut the machine down, cursing the ageing equipment. Just as well it had held long enough to cover up the worst of Loki's crime.

'What are you doing? You stupid girl!' Dad's voice boomed across the field from ten rows down.

Damn it. Couldn't he have stayed away for a while longer? 'Seeder's blown a hose,' she called out.

'Well, didn't you just service it?' he demanded as he stalked closer.

Yes, the seeder, the tractor, and the ute, all while Googling with a dodgy internet connection for parts that had last been shipped in on the Ark. 'The hose has perished.'

'Then you'd better bloody fix it and quick.'

'It'll take days to come from our usual supplier. I still have a few hectares to seed. I can't wait that long.' Better to let him make the suggestion about going into town. If she did, he'd kick up a fuss.

His bushy eyebrows knitted together in a scowl. She hadn't seen him smile in eight years, and several years before that. She wasn't sure he knew how to.

'Better go into town and see if that useless lot at the hardware store have got one.'

Fat chance. Noah probably sold the last one before the Big Flood. And by her dad's estimation, everyone was useless or stupid. His constant negativity and denigration dragged at her will to stay positive.

'Good idea, Dad.'

'And hurry up about it. You're wasting good daylight hours. We don't have many left before winter sets in.'

As if it were her fault he wouldn't buy new equipment and she spent more time fixing what they had than working it. 'I'll go clean up. Did you want anything from town?'

That earned her a disdainful look as he turned to walk away. 'Just get the bloody hose fixed and get on with the God damn job. Time is money and you're wasting both.'

Tameka ignored the shaft of rejection that closed her throat. She'd never be good enough, no matter how hard she worked. She should just walk away. Get in the ute and drive, leave down the same road her mum had taken.

But her mother had taught her to respect her elders. Her father's rule was absolute no matter how much she disagreed or wanted otherwise. This time he was right, she was wasting time even thinking about how things could be different.

She'd lost count of the times she'd thought about walking away, telling him to shove his farm and work it himself. And she hated herself for not having the guts to set off into the unknown alone for the cold, hard fear that what she'd face outside of Wongan Creek would be worse.

She'd never see Harley again if she did go, or watch her seeds grow into a field of barley, and her dad would die in a place that was falling down around his ears. Even though she sometimes thought he deserved to, she didn't want to have her father's death on her conscience too. It was bad enough that she was to blame for everything that had happened on Golden Acres to date.

Harley cradled his ribs and winced as Tameka's ute bounced over another bump in the road that felt the size of a mountain and jarred the length of his spine.

'Jesus, Tikki. Take it easy. When do you plan to change the shocks on this thing?'

'The next time Marty McFly and Doc Brown come to town in the DeLorean and bring a new set with them. And don't call me that.'

There was a time when he'd laugh and tickle her ribs for being cheeky. A time long gone now. 'They'd better hurry it up before all the panels shake off the frame.'

She cast him a quick side glance before turning her concentration back to the road. 'Would you prefer to walk?'

'You offered me a ride.'

A pink blush crept into her cheeks. Oh yes, he

thought, she remembered that line. He'd bet his last standing bine of hops that she remembered how that ride had gone down too. Before her dad had almost ripped the door of Harley's ute off its hinges.

But this time his cockiness didn't raise a smile, nor did she slip her hand to his thigh and let it follow a path up to his … well, the part of him that was paying full attention to the direction of his thoughts, thank you very much.

He cleared his throat and shifted, cranking down the window to let some cool air in. He let his arm rest on top of the brittle window seals around the frame.

Tameka and her dad didn't seem to be faring too well either if the state of the burst hose lying on the floor at his feet and the ute were anything to go by.

There was a difference between neglect and well-loved when it came to equipment. Tikki's was well-loved with the need of a cash injection. One the Chalmers clearly didn't have these days.

'Can I buy you a late lunch at Mama Bella's Cafe?' She got skinnier every time he saw her.

'This isn't a date, Harley. It's business. We'll go talk to your dad then I'll sort out my hose, bring you home and we can go back to not talking to each other over the fence. I'll get on with my business and you can get on with yours.'

Ouch. She still had the power to cut him off at the

balls. So, no peace treaty then, not even a brief one. Had he really believed there could be?

'Cool. Just wanted to … you know … say thank you?'

She sighed, her knuckles white on the worn steering wheel. 'This is what neighbours do. They stand by each other in times of need and then get on with their lives when the crisis has passed.'

Direct hit. When Louis Chalmers had locked himself and his daughter away, the community had offered to help, only to have their hands bitten for their trouble. He'd tried to reach her, multiple times, but each time he'd hit a hundred-and-twenty-kilogram brick wall in the shape of her father holding a loaded shotgun.

Then the ultimate insult had come. Two days after the Big Bang, Chalmers had cut off their water supply from the dam the farms had shared for four generations with the Fishers, the previous owners of Golden Acres. Not exactly how neighbours stood by each other.

'I tried to see you.' Harley tapped out a rhythm on the door panel with his fingers.

'I know you did.' Her hands relaxed a little on the wheel.

'Your father threatened to shoot me if I came anywhere near you.'

She grimaced. 'That sounds about right. Just as well you didn't test out his threat.'

'Yeah, Dad thought it was wise to listen to him. It didn't stop me wanting to though.'

'You did the right thing by staying away. Maybe things were happening too fast for us anyway. I don't know. If Mum was still here ...' Her words trailed away to silence.

He wanted to ask if she'd ever heard from her mum again, but old wounds festered enough without re-opening them. Rumours had flown around town, but no-one had confirmed anything. Mai Chalmers had simply packed her suitcase and left right after the Big Bang.

And knowing Chalmers the way they did, no-one had questioned her leaving because they thought it served the bastard right for treating her the way he did. Everyone had wondered though, at least once, why she hadn't taken her daughter with her ... until they'd found another Wongan Creek disaster to focus on.

The town centre loomed ahead, and Tameka eased the ute down Main Street at the required limit of forty kilometres per hour. Harley felt her stiffen as she scanned the pavement outside the shops, her knuckles white from gripping the steering.

'Which way to your folks' place?'

'Left at Addie Street, two blocks down and hook a right into Sunrise Terrace. Number eighty-eight. You don't have to do this, Tameka. We can get your hose and leave. I'll talk to Dad later.'

'No. I owe it to him. To you. To anyone else who

may be affected. Damn it, Harley, this sucks. I tried to tell him.' She pulled up outside number eighty-eight, turned off the engine and sat with her hands balled into fists in her lap, controlling the in and out whoosh of her breath.

Harley frowned. What on earth was she afraid of? Tameka had never been afraid of anything. 'It's Mum and Dad's place, not a lion's den. They care about you. Always have.'

'I know that, smart-arse.'

'Then what are you worried about?'

'The questions. Always the questions.'

She took a deep breath and let it out slowly. And damn it, he wanted to deposit a kiss on that beautiful mouth to see if she tasted as good as he remembered, and chase her fears away, fix some of the shit he'd caused that had driven this wedge between them.

'Mine or theirs?'

'Everyone's.'

Chapter Four

Tameka pushed open the door of the ute, got out and slammed it shut behind her. She cursed the speed with which Harley's long legs covered the distance between them and the look of concern on his face. She didn't need him worrying about her.

'Step aside, Baker.'

'Not until I'm sure you can handle walking up the pathway to the front door without falling apart. Like your machinery.' He pointed to the hydraulic hose now lying on the dashboard of her ute where he'd put it.

She pushed past him and headed for the gate, ignoring the tentacles of anxiety that wrapped themselves around her chest and squeezed. 'I'm fine.' She hadn't fallen apart for a long time. Couldn't afford to.

'And I call bullshit on that.' The quiet certainty in his voice almost had her crumbling.

Turning to face him, she edged her chin higher. 'You don't know anything about me, Harley. You haven't for almost a decade.' Damn, it hurt to know that was the truth and that he had no idea of the mess her life had become. No clue how messed up her thought processes and loyalties were. No need to know that she had to be strong and weak at the same time, paused between fight or flight, give up or survive.

Tameka eyed him from under the brim of the hat she'd slapped on her head. He stood tall, strong, and solid, feet apart in dusty leather work boots, jeans clinging to his thighs, his hands firmly on his hips.

She wanted to run into those arms and be held against his heartbeat until all the nightmares of the last eight years disappeared. But she wasn't nineteen anymore, and Harley was as out of reach as the moon and stars.

Over his shoulder she spotted Harley's mum rushing up the road towards them, a grin on her lips and a large brown paper bag in her hand. Her blue eyes, so like her son's, sparkled warmly, her free arm already reaching out for the hug Harley received and returned with equal enthusiasm before setting his mum back on her feet.

Tameka watched the embrace with her heart in her throat. It had been so long since someone had hugged her like that.

'Darling, you made it … and, Tameka, what a lovely surprise to see you here too.'

'Hello, Mrs Baker.'

Tameka blinked back the sudden prick of tears. Warmth was the last thing she'd expected from Harley's mum after the whole scene over the dam and her father virtually cutting off the Bakers' livelihood. But the aftershocks of Shirley Baker's sunny enthusiasm were hard to ignore. She had the kind of smile a person couldn't help but return, no matter how much sadness was locked away in their heart.

'I've been in to pick up a cake from Mama Bella's for tea. Your dad is so excited about you coming to visit. He's curious to know how the harvest went and how the crops in the greenhouses are doing.'

Tameka shivered. She hated having to be the one to dull the happy light that shone in Shirley Baker's eyes. When would the Chalmers stop hurting the Bakers? So many nights, lying in the dark, on edge at every noise, she wished things could be different. That she could turn back the past and change the future.

'We've got a lot to talk about, Mum. That's why Tameka came in with me to see Dad.' The seriousness in Harley's tone did nothing to dampen his mum's enthusiasm.

Releasing her son, Shirley Baker stepped back, her smile brightening. 'You came in together? That's great!'

She hugged Tameka hard. 'Sweetheart, it's so lovely to see you again. It's been ages.'

Oh, hell no, she couldn't let Mrs Baker think this was a reconciliation. Not when she was about to bring more heartache to their table. 'I had to come into town for some spare parts. When Harley told me he was coming to see you, I offered him a lift.'

Lamer than Baby's excuse for carrying watermelons in *Dirty Dancing*, she thought, but damn it, she wasn't anywhere near ready to let go of the warmth of Mrs Baker's welcome just yet to reveal the true reason for her visit.

'Oh, that's lovely, dear.' Shirley shook her head sadly. 'The mood in town is a little unpleasant today. A couple of the farmers came in complaining about spray drift damage to their crops. It happens every year. There's plenty of talk about selling out to John Bannister. The changing weather conditions and expanding mine operations is making it harder and harder to maintain farming land.'

'I hope Dad's not stressing out about it too much, Mum. He can't afford to after the last heart attack.' Harley placed an arm around his mother's shoulders.

'You know your dad, love. He can't help himself.' A frown crossed Shirley's brow. 'A word of warning since you're in town, Tameka. It wouldn't be fair not to let you know you might run into some angry farmers while you're here. Your father's name has been rolled around already this morning. He's the only one left using the phenoxies that caused the damage.'

She should have known it was a mistake coming into town. Tameka let her shoulders sag as the urge to run and hide clawed at her belly.

Damn the questions and the answers and damn her father to hell for his insistence on using such archaic, destructive methods of weed control. Damn him too for leaving her to face the fall out while he buried his head in a bottle.

'Great. Just great.' She caught the look of confusion on Shirley's face at her abrupt tone. 'Thanks for the heads-up. How is Mr Baker?'

'Oh, he's okay, sweetheart. As well as can be expected. Even though he's not involved in the farm with Harley running it, he still likes to keep an eye on these things.' Shirley patted Tameka's hand. 'He's going to love seeing you. You are coming in, aren't you? It's been too long.'

The tug at Tameka's heart came close to pain. She liked Harley's parents. Their home life had always been so unified compared to her own. Harley had a string of uncles, aunts, and cousins — blood relations or otherwise — whereas Tameka didn't even know where her mother was from in Vietnam.

Mum had seldom spoken of her home or her life before she'd met Tameka's father.

Khong co van de con. Toi o day. Chau Uc. No matter, child. I am here. Australia.

His parents were always doing things within the community while her own had cut themselves off from everyone, including their neighbours. Only Tameka, Harley and his brother, Ryan, had formed a bond of friendship, the way only children could amidst the adversity between the adults.

Her breath hitched at the thought of Ryan. Gone so long ago, way too soon, far too young. Ryan's death had brought her and Harley closer as he'd struggled to come to terms with the fact that his brother would never swim in the dam or play football in the fields with them again. That too had changed as they grew, and friendship had morphed into a relationship between her and Harley.

Even in the worst crisis, the Bakers stuck together like a family should, unlike the Chalmers. Who knew where Dad's family was? So far she hadn't found anything on the Chalmers' ancestry. And Mum ... well, she'd never know. All her research had turned up were dead ends.

No marriage certificate, no passport, no papers, no trace of where her mother had come from. And the internet search engines threw up thousands of Nguyens — a dynasty rather than a family name.

'Tameka?' Shirley squeezed her hand. 'Are you okay, sweetheart?'

No, she wasn't okay at all. She missed normal — the warm hugs, the hot soup in winter at Mrs Baker's kitchen table, the fun, friendship, laughter, and comfort in Harley's arms.

'Yes, all good.' Leaning in, she kissed Shirley's cheek. 'Do you mind if I go inside and have a word with Mr B about the spray drift? Since he's on the council at the National Farmers Federation, I'd like to get some advice on how to deal with the situation.'

'Of course, sweetheart, go ahead. He'll be happy to discuss things with you and help you work out a resolution beneficial to everyone.'

If only her father would adopt the same approach. Tameka crossed her arms over her chest and tried to ease the tightness that held her breathing captive.

'I'll come with you.' Harley stepped forward.

'No, it's okay. I need to handle this on my own.'

'Tikki —'

'I *said* I can do this alone.' She hadn't meant for the bite in her tone to slip out and regretted the cloud of hurt that formed then dissipated in Harley's eyes.

'Fine.'

She read the warning in his gaze, but she had no intention of putting Tom Baker at risk of another heart attack and knew she'd have to tread carefully around the subject.

It wasn't her place to tell his father about the extent

of the damage on Bakers Hill, only to fix the mess she'd created. If only she knew how.

Shirley's gaze flicked between them. 'Harley and I will be in the kitchen making tea. Come through when you're done.' Shirley squeezed Tameka's arm. 'It's not your fault. We understand that.'

It was her fault because she couldn't stop it, but no-one would understand that. Ever. 'Thank you,' she whispered then she walked away because if she spent any longer out there surrounded by motherly comfort and love, she'd give in to the tears of regret that lodged in her throat.

Mrs B's words followed her up the gravel pathway to the front door. 'Such a shame we don't see enough of her since … well, you know. She's such a lovely girl.'

She wished she were that girl Harley's mum thought her to be. The girl she had been once. The one who'd been carefree and full of dreams, full of hope for the future … instead of the empty shell she'd become.

'Oh, Harley, she's so skinny.' His mum whispered the words between them as Tameka disappeared into the house. 'Is she okay? Do you think she's eating well enough?'

Harley grinned. If he said no, Mum would produce a

truckload of takeaway containers filled with leftovers to give to Tameka. If he said yes, she'd call his bluff. Either way, he'd end up with a cooler full of food and his freezer would be overflowing because he doubted a Chalmers would take anything from a Baker. Not even a home-cooked meal.

'I'm sure she's fine, Mum,' he said, even though he was worried too. 'You remember how tiny and delicate her mum was. Tameka takes after her in build, that's all.'

'I don't know, Harley. Something doesn't feel right. It never has. That was such a terrible business with her mum leaving and all the hoo-hah over the dam.' Shirley sighed. 'I don't understand why she stayed with that awful man and didn't go with her mum. Do you think she's happy? She looks so sad and terribly tired.'

Sad and empty, a shell of the girl he'd once known. It made his heart ache for her. And he understood even less why she'd stayed with Louis Chalmers when she'd had the perfect excuse to leave. Harley would have taken her into his home in a heartbeat.

One day she would leave, and he'd never see her again, a thought that scared the bloody life out of him. Then he would have to let go of the hope that one day they might get back together again. And he wasn't anywhere near ready to let go of that chance, slim though it might be.

'Sowing season is a busy time of the year for her, Mum. She's got plenty to worry about. Too much or too little rain, frost, weeds, damage from the bloody parrots that chew everything including the pipes on the machinery. Those damn things chomp right through the bitumen on the roads, never mind the damage they do to the crops. Once her barley is established, she'll catch a break.'

'You'll keep an eye on her, won't you, Harley?'

'Always.'

'Good because I worry about that girl. How could Mai go off without her? It's so sad.'

Harley put an arm around his mum's shoulders and hugged her. 'You forget, Mum, Tameka's one tough cookie.' Sometimes a little too tough for his liking. 'Now tell me, how's Dad really doing?'

'He's okay. I've tried to keep him as calm as possible over all this talk of everyone selling out to John Bannister. I think he's worried the whole town will become one big hole in the ground if we don't take a stand against the expansion of the mine and persevere with farming. We need more people like old Harry Murchison. He told Bannister to take a hike and now he's building a retirement facility.' She smiled and winked. 'Although no-one dares refer to it as that. Harry insists it's a lifestyle village.' She sighed. 'So much speculation and rumour at the moment. Anyway, I'm sure your dad's waiting for his tea. Oh, he'll be so happy to see you now you're done with harvest. It's such a busy time.'

'I think he misses it.' Harley smiled as he glanced at the front door. How was Tameka doing with his dad? Would the added stress put more strain on his heart?

After the heart attack, Dad had been banned from taking part in the harvest. He hadn't accepted it quietly and only Mum's insistence that they move to town, closer to the hospital, had convinced him to give in. No-one argued with Shirley Baker when her size sixes were firmly down.

'He was in the pub earlier today to catch up on the gossip. Louis Chalmers' spray drift has caused extensive damage. Travis Bailey was one of the lucky ones. His canola is mostly unaffected.'

Harley's heart sank. 'That's good news for Travis.'

'But not for you, right?' She hooked her arm through his and urged him forward. 'You would have been directly in the path of the drift.'

He matched his stride to hers as they walked towards the front door. *Bugger.* 'You've been a farmer's wife too long, Mum. You know too much. Three hectares of bines copped the worst of it. And to add to the devastation, the whole crop in the north paddock has downy mildew eating away the cones. I don't know how to tell Dad without the risk of upsetting him.'

More stress was the last thing any of them needed. First the floods, then the drought, Ryan's death, the Big

Bang, the water crisis and then the heart attack — Dad had enough to deal with over the years without adding this latest stumbling block.

'He's already guessed, Harley. He knows the risk. It's how bad the damage is that we'll have to shoulder. What does Tameka have to say about it?'

'She says she's tried to talk Chalmers out of using phenoxy-based herbicides.' Harley ran a hand through his hair. 'We both know her father can be a stubborn old codger.'

'That and more. What sort of loss are we looking at, son?'

'Around twenty thousand dollars per hectare. We have three hectares of crop damage along the Golden Acres border and another five in the top paddock with partial phenoxy damage and the rest down with disease.'

'Plus, the cost of the modifications we had to do when Chalmers cut off the water supply.'

'I was banking on this crop to pay off at least a third of that cost.'

'What about the mung beans?'

'Not mature enough to yield a decent, profitable harvest yet.'

She stopped walking and looked up at him, her forehead creased in a frown. 'Bakers Hill will make it through this, won't it, son? It will break your father's heart if we have to let it go.'

Oh Jesus, he hoped so. 'Of course it will. It has to.

I've arranged a meeting with Greg Saunders at the bank, Mum. As soon as I have a plan together to present, he'll go in to bat for us. He knows we're good for it. I'm sure he can hold off the dogs for a while until I sort something out.' For Dad's sake, he had to make sure he did.

Chapter Five

At least Tom Baker had taken the news well and come up with some helpful solutions to her issues with weed control. The rest of the town didn't appear to be as forgiving.

Tameka waited at the counter and pretended to ignore the whispers and sometimes not-so-quiet digs about her father's farming methods while Harley cruised the shelves and chatted with the handful of people in the hardware store.

She shivered. How easily people turned on their own when they had a fire lit under their arse. Not that her father didn't deserve the censure. He'd cost a lot of people money this harvest and probably the years before that too. And she was as much to blame as he was, powerless to stop him as she'd watched the crop duster sweep the fields and a haze of minute, damaging particles drift on the wind.

Not even Tom Baker's quiet reassurance and sound advice could stop the frustration from crawling through her. Nothing would work unless she could convince her father to see the truth about the damage his phenoxies were causing.

She dropped her gaze to her boots as yet another patron glared at her on his way past to the feed section. On the rare occasion she did come into Wongan Creek for supplies, she avoided contact with the townsfolk as much as possible. They were nice people, but their curiosity only made old wounds fester and their questions hurt too much to answer — particularly the question that everyone would ask if they knew how bad her dad really was. The one she couldn't find the answer to herself. *Why don't you leave?* So, she ignored their kindness that threatened the wall she'd built to keep them out.

Today she hadn't needed that barrier. They'd been the ones to ignore her. First old Mal serving behind the counter then his wife Ahn on the cash register. None of their usual smiles and cheerful hellos. It wasn't until Travis Bailey and Harry Murchison walked in that she'd actually been acknowledged.

Harry tapped his cane on the counter. 'What's wrong with you, you miserable old bastard? Can't you see the girl needs help?'

'Don't serve her kind here.'

'What *kind* is that exactly? A customer who wants to spend money in your store?'

'Her father's done a lot of damage in this town.'

Harry looked around. 'I don't see her bloody father here now, do you? All I see is a girl with a hose in her hand that needs fixing.'

Warmth covered Tameka's back and Harley's hand came to rest at her waist. She let out a long breath and clutched the hose tightly, her fingers white as the gentle tone of his voice washed over her.

'I came to see what's taking so long. Everything okay, Tikki?'

'It will be as soon as Mal here gets his head out his arse,' Harry muttered.

'Terrible place for a head to be. Hey, Travis. How are you, mate?'

Travis leaned across Harry and shook Harley's hand. 'All good. Lucky we stopped by. Harry needed some sheep poo for the garden.'

Harley shifted behind her as he held out a hand to Harry too. 'I would've thought your sheep did enough of that, Harry.'

'Buggers keep running off across the creek and doing it in Liv Waterman's vineyard.'

'They're probably chasing her latest vintage. I heard it's a good drop.' He eased the broken hose out of Tameka's hand and placed it on the counter in front of Mal. 'Can I get one of those made up, please, mate?'

Tameka resisted the urge to sink back into his solid warmth. Kindness. Friendship. Two staple foods in the diet of life. Something she hadn't had since … well since Harley.

With a mutter about Judases under his breath, Mal took the hose and disappeared, leaving Ahn to smile awkwardly at Tameka. She smiled back, trying desperately to add warmth and ignore the resentment that flooded her. She turned her head to look at Harley, her gaze finding his. 'Thank you.'

In another time and place, she would have felt his arm slide around her shoulders and pull her into his embrace, the warmth of his body against hers and the surge of love for him in her heart. Those days were gone. Had been for a long time. She wasn't his girl anymore, never would be again.

She stepped aside and waited for Mal to return with the hose, thumbs hooked into the pockets of her jeans, hip leaning against the counter and one booted foot toeing the stained concrete floor. Travis and Harley chatted about footy and avoided the topic of crops and spray drift while Harry kept a close eye on Mal. The whisperers and gossips dispersed. The store echoed with silence again except for Harley and Travis' voices, and the clatter of Mal's tools as he threw them around his bench making her hose.

Tameka couldn't blame him for his anger or resentment. Her father wasn't exactly a town favourite, never had been. Mal walked back and dropped the new hose on the counter, complete with new brass fittings.

'Thank you, Mal. How much do I owe you?' She reached into her pocket for her wallet.

Mal glanced over her head at Harley before wiping away imaginary sawdust from the counter top. 'Nothing. Take it. Just stop … stop spraying that shit, okay?'

'I'm working on it.' She stilled the movement of his hands with hers, making him meet her gaze. 'I promise. Thanks for the hose.' Damn it, she hoped that one day she could keep that promise. She let go of Mal's hand and turned to Harley. 'Ready to go when you are.' Tameka leaned over and kissed Harry's cheek. 'Thank you, Harry.'

Harry blushed and rubbed his cheek. 'Been a long time since a girl kissed my cheek. Might have to play hero more often.'

Travis grinned. 'And all the girls in Wongan Creek between eighteen and a hundred are breathing a sigh of relief right now that by tomorrow you will have forgotten that promise.'

Harry snorted. 'Smart-arse. I'm old, not dead. Yet.'

Harley chuckled. 'Nice to see you both again. We've got to rush.' He paused, hands on his hips, drawing Tameka's attention to his long fingers resting against the faded denim. 'Mum's worried Tameka's too skinny.

She's prepped a year's worth of food to take home so we'd best head out and get it into the freezer.'

Tameka rolled her eyes against the tug at her heart. She'd like nothing more than to sit at the kitchen table and wolf down a meal that didn't taste like the dried out remains of something that shouldn't be microwaved. It wasn't that she couldn't cook, more that she had to cook what Dad liked the way he liked it or pay the consequences. And no way would Dad have Shirley Baker's food in his freezer, so she'd have to find a way of persuading Harley to keep it for himself.

'I'm surprised she didn't make you stay for dinner too then.' Travis laughed. 'Shirley's meals are epic.'

'She tried. It was tempting, but there'd be more leftovers and we've got enough in the back of the ute to keep us going and still feed the whole region.'

'And I've got to get back before the light goes or I won't be able to fix the seeder for tomorrow,' Tameka reminded him.

'We'll get home in time, I promise. Even if my stomach growls all the way.' He tipped his head closer to hers to deliver the words in a low and sexy baritone that skimmed along her skin leaving goosebumps in its wake. 'You're my ride, Tikki. I need you.'

What she needed was to get home fast, away from this contact that made her want what she couldn't have. She placed a firm hand on Harley's chest and forced him to take a step back. 'Guess you'll have to go hungry then. See ya.'

She pressed her way between Harley and Harry, and headed for the door, pushing her way out into the late afternoon sunshine. She didn't get far before Harley caught up.

'We could grab a takeaway burger from Mama Bella's on the way out?'

Tameka stopped at the driver's door of her ute and dragged off her hat, tossing it onto the seat through the open window. 'Jesus, Baker! Is food all you think of?'

His eyes slammed into hers with all the force of Luke Skywalker's light sabre and ripped her heart in two. 'Not *all*, no.'

She held his gaze for a moment until the heat and want got too hot to handle then she opened the door. 'Get in or walk.' She slid behind the wheel and cranked the engine until the starter motor screamed in protest.

Harley winced as he got in and fastened his seatbelt.

'Shut up.' She put the car in reverse and backed out of the parking space.

'Didn't say a word.'

He leaned an elbow on the open window and hooked his fingers into the rain channel on the roof. His free hand rested on his knee, a little too close to the gearstick for her comfort. Selecting first gear would be a problem with his hand in the way.

She tried hard not to let her fingers brush his as she

moved the gearstick, but his legs were so damn long, and his hands were so bloody big, and it felt like he was all over the freaking cabin. She should have let him drive so that she could curl as far away from him into the corner as possible.

Silence stretched between them as Wongan Creek disappeared from her rear-view mirror. Harley took his elbow off the window and leaned forward to take the hydraulic hose off the dashboard. He flexed it between his hands, softening the stiff rubber. Great. At least his hands were away from the gearstick but, bloody hell, the movement of those fingers on the hose as he made it into something pliable was damn distracting.

Turn up the music. That would kill the tension in the air. Tameka leaned forward and twisted the knob on the radio until Keith Urban's voice drowned out all thought in her head and had every cow and sheep in the passing paddocks lifting their head to see what the fuss was all about.

Harley cast a look in her direction. She ignored it, gripped the wheel, and found a pothole in the road to bounce over.

'Pull over.' He grunted as the next bump felt more like a mountain.

'No.'

'Pull. Over.' His growl rose as Keith's voice faded. 'Now.' He snapped the radio off, but his voice softened.

'Please, Tikki. Before I end up in traction with a spinal injury.'

She pulled into a rest stop under the shade of a eucalyptus tree. She'd barely dragged up the handbrake before Harley was out of the ute, around the bonnet and opening her door.

'Out.'

The word was quiet and gentle, not shouted like she'd expect it to be if he was angry. Because, Jesus, the last thing she needed in her life was another angry man. 'Why?'

He dragged a hand through his hair, leaned across her and unclipped her seat belt, his arm brushing across her chest. She sucked in a breath at the contact.

'Out or I'll have to pick you up and carry you.' A little teasing mixed into the irritation in his tone.

Oh, hell no because that meant being held up against him right where she wanted to be and couldn't afford the cost. She shoved him away and got out, slamming the door closed behind her and leaning back against it, crossing her arms under her breasts.

'What? You're making me late, Baker.'

'What's crawled up your arse?'

He reached his arm past her head and gripped the roof, bringing his face a little closer to hers, a move that should have felt invasive, should have put her on edge, but didn't because this was Harley and she'd never been afraid of him.

And damn it, that made her want to lean into him and just feel. Him, his heartbeat, his warmth, and everything that was safe and secure about him as it had been in the past when he'd been her haven.

'Mine? What's crawled up yours?' She poked at his chest, warmth shimmying up through her fingertip.

'You've been on edge since we got to town.'

'So? I don't like coming into town. Is that a crime?'

She drew in a breath as his hands found her hips and anchored her in front of him. Her feet itched to run, to climb back in the ute and drive, and leave him at the side of the road if she had to.

She didn't want Harley poking around in her thoughts and discovering the fear that lived inside her. Not him. Nobody. Ever. Because the truth would shake this town so hard, the aftershocks would be felt all the way to Tasmania.

'And what do you know about me anyway? What does it matter to you?' The snipe in her tone made her shudder. Harley was the last person in the world who deserved it even if they weren't friends anymore.

'You matter. You always have.'

The quiet conviction in his words was her undoing. The effort to hold back her emotions burnt at the back of her throat. He drew her closer, a gentle tug that her body accepted but her mind rejected. She didn't want to be plastered up against the man she'd been forbidden to keep yet wanted with every pixel of her obliterated soul because he was the only one who could put her back together again.

And there was all this heat still between them and the warmth of his denims against hers where their bodies still fit perfectly even after all this time apart.

'Damn you, Baker.'

The bastard grinned. A cheeky, confident, knowing grin that took the edge off the irritation that swirled in her belly. He tipped up her chin, searching her face, his eyes seeing right through her tough exterior. She stared at the cleft in his because meeting his eyes would have her unravelling like a ball of wool in the paws of a kitten.

Then his head dipped, and his lips were on hers, a sweet memory of the last time they'd been in that exact same spot. God, he tasted good — like forbidden fruit, wickedly smooth chocolate, or a really good home brew, and just as heady.

But his mouth didn't stay closed long enough to enjoy the drunken effects of his kiss. Or to forget why he'd kissed her in the first place. A trick he'd used before when times were different, and it had been all about discovery not distraction.

'Now we've got that out of the way, what's got ants in your pants, Tikki?' He drew his head back a little.

Not far enough out of the way. She could still feel his breath whisper across her mouth. 'It's the pitying looks and unasked questions, as well the voiced ones. And now they've added anger and resentment too.'

'They care.' His hands played in soothing circles on her back. 'We all do. You're so unreachable now.'

She traced the pattern on his shirt with her fingertips. 'It's the way it needs to be.'

How could she tell him that she longed for the old days when life was easier, and her dad was simply a narcissistic bastard rather than the angry, violent drunk he'd become?

That his mood swings grew worse every day. How he prowled the property like a caged tiger waiting to pounce on its prey and tear it to pieces, and she feared she'd be that prey.

That if she left him like her mother did, he'd take his shotgun and blow his head off after downing a bottle of Jacks — neat, straight from the neck of the bottle, no glass necessary — and she couldn't let him do that no matter how much of an arsehole he was. Even though a part of her wished he would.

How every night, she took the gun from the side of his chair once he'd fallen asleep, removed the bullets and locked them in the gun safe only to find it reloaded the next morning. A ticking time bomb that could have her cleaning up shit and blood and brains off the walls and floor at any moment unless they were hers instead. How there were days she'd welcome having to take a bucket and hot water and do just that for the peace and freedom it would bring.

But here, in Harley's arms again, the edge of reason blurred. She leaned her head against his heart and listened to the strong, steady rhythm.

Without the noise of the town around them, she heard the birds in the trees chirping away as the mild warmth of a day that promised another long, lonely, cold winter faded and the chill of evening crept in. Then she'd have to face the horror that darkness brought again, the circle of a life she could never escape. Every God damn night.

Tameka squeezed her eyes shut and breathed in the essence of Harley, a comfort she'd take home with her and hold close tonight as she waited for the inevitable.

'I've got to go.'

His arms closed around her, and he hugged her tight. 'I know.' With a kiss to her crown and a sigh that echoed through her own chest, he released her. 'I'll drive.'

Chapter Six

'Where the hell have you been?' Dad, angrier and more drunk than usual, staggered into the homestead doorway as she slammed the door closed on the ute. *Great.*

'I had to wait for the hose. I'm going to fit it now and then get dinner for you.'

'Well, you'd better bloody get a move on, girl. I'm hungry.' He stamped back into the house, his footsteps echoing down the empty hallway.

Hungry and angry so that he could push the food around his plate and bitch that it wasn't hot enough, too salty or tasted like ten-day-old dog food. She could serve up caviar and Moet, and it still wouldn't be good enough.

It had always been that way. Even while her mum

was there. He'd been grumpy and quick-tempered over little things and picky about food.

Tameka had disappointed him in so many ways. She wasn't a boy. She couldn't cook for shit. As a farmer, she was pretty average. And when he'd caught her screwing Harley Baker, her mother had left her father. An unforgivable sin that had nothing at all to do with the way he treated his wife when she failed to produce the son he was so obsessed with having. On the very edge of reason that made no sense at all. Nothing about the way life had turned out made sense.

According to him, they were the cause of all his heartache, the reason for all his failures. A bad daughter and a terrible wife even when they'd tried so hard to be good ones.

Running the hose through her hands, she thought how not so long ago Harley's hands had been on the rubber, on her hips and back. How in that one short moment, she'd felt the stirring of being human again. Of being able to feel something other than resentment, defeat, and the ache of loss.

But Harley was next door doing his own thing and he wasn't hers any longer. All she had was her dream, one that could never come true.

As she fitted the hose to the seeder, topped up the hydraulic oil in the tank and tested the pressure, she thought on her pipedream about the organic vegetables she'd grow in a section of the field and the greenhouses she could build.

She could restore the gardens to what they'd once been and turn the homestead into a cooking school where she could create the tasty, imaginative dishes she wanted to for an appreciative audience.

For now, she was a guardian for the land she loved so much. She couldn't leave, not with the hope in her heart that one day she might inherit it and make that dream come true. She had nowhere else to go. No family, no friends, no future to make her feet walk the road out of Wongan Creek.

This was the only job she'd ever had. Living in the city held no appeal. She belonged on the land where she could get her hands dirty and see the fruits of her efforts sprouting from the soil.

Loki's excited bark reached her ears. Tameka raised her head to watch the dog chase down the rope Harley tossed for him. Harley lifted a hand in a wave. She didn't return it. Best not to encourage him to think that today's slip of judgement on her part could lead to their friendship, or anything else, being rekindled.

She tucked the wrench into her back pocket and wiped her hands on the rag she'd left on the seat of the seeder. With one last look at Harley, she turned her back on him and walked away to the house.

She'd like nothing more than a shower and some alone time, but Dad wouldn't have the patience for that.

She needed to get some food into him, so he wasn't running on alcohol fumes alone.

In the kitchen, Tameka opened the freezer and studied the meagre contents. Her food budget didn't stretch far, and since Dad refused to support the local grocer in Wongan Creek, she had to make a monthly run to Perth.

The temptation to keep driving when she made those trips … but Dad would find her and bring her back if she did, no doubt about it. And the consequences wouldn't be worth it.

This late in the month they were running low on everything. She liked to cook, to create, but Dad wasn't exactly an appreciative recipient of anything that wasn't the standard fare of overcooked meat, pasta, and potatoes.

The menu tonight would be spaghetti bolognaise or shepherd's pie because all she had left was mince, pasta, and potatoes. She pulled out the packet of meat and tossed it into the microwave to defrost, thinking of all the food still in the back of the ute after Harley had taken his share, despite her insistence he take it all. Food that would go to waste because she couldn't bring it to the table. Dad would never eat it. His mood meant she'd be cleaning most of anything she presented off the floor anyway when he lost his shit and threw the plate down.

What turned an already angry man so bitter? She'd searched for the answers through boxes stored in the shed out back but found no explanation for the lack of family photos or clues to his past.

Unlike almost everyone in Wongan Creek, he hadn't grown up here. He'd arrived in the district an older man with his pregnant, much younger wife in tow. She'd heard the stories, the whispers about how he'd come by his Vietnamese wife.

He'd stayed out of the community, only interacting with the Bakers and even that relationship had been tenuous. If it hadn't been for Mum and Shirley Baker having the odd cuppa together and the fact the family had shared the dam's water supply, there probably wouldn't have been a friendship at all. Louis Chalmers didn't have friends, he had associates. And even those were few.

Tameka sighed as she put a pan on the cooktop and lit the gas, going through the motions to cook the meal. Truth was her dad was a bit of a mystery man.

He never talked about his family or his childhood, and he'd never been the kind of father to spend time with his child. He'd barely spoken to Mum or her unless it was to deliver an order. A man so far removed from society's version of a father, he might as well not be human. Sometimes he wasn't.

She dropped handfuls of spaghetti into a pot of boiling water on the back burner and stirred it. The heavy thump of boots moved down the hallway to the kitchen.

'What the fuck is taking you so long? Can't you even cook a bloody meal, you stupid girl?'

'It'll be ready soon, Dad. I've only just started it. Why don't you go sit in the lounge room and I'll bring it through when it's ready? The news will be on.' She turned from the cooktop to face him.

'Don't bloody patronise me, girl. I don't want to watch the God damn news. I want to eat.'

His breath reeked of a mixture of stale and fresh booze as he shouted the words in her face. Tameka's stomach dropped at the angry tone and rough grip on her arm. She'd be wearing bruises tomorrow. What scared her more than the anger was the drunken crazy in his eyes, intensified since the last time.

'It's almost ready.' Heat from the open flame licked at her skin as he backed her up against the range.

'I want it now.'

'Okay, okay.' Tameka held up the spoon she'd been using to stir the spaghetti between them. 'Please let go of my arm, Dad. I'll give you your food now.' The heat at her back became a sting and the smell of burning filled her nose. 'Dad, you need to step back, please. My shirt has caught on the flame.'

She tried to keep her voice calm even when a scream built in her throat as the hot edge of the pan bit into her back and fingers of flame scratched at her skin.

He raised his hand, palm up. She pulled back to avoid the slap she saw coming, the pan behind her went flying, the bottle of oil fell over as it connected, and the open flame flared.

Tameka staggered sideways, dropped on the floor, and rolled to kill the flames that ate at her back. She prayed he'd come to his senses and reach for the fire extinguisher as she lay in the kitchen doorway with her back stinging. Instead, the steel cap of his boot connected hard with her temple as he stepped over her and walked away.

Pain seared through her head and back. The flames grew higher over the cooktop, dancing and licking at the walls as she rolled over onto her side and her world faded away.

Harley rubbed at the headache behind his eyes. The cost of the damaged crop had tipped Bakers Hill into the red so far it would take him two seasons to recover it. And now with the additional cost of new rhizomes added in for next year and a crop that wouldn't reach maturity for a while, the future looked pretty dismal. He should be angry with Tameka for continuing the practice of using herbicides, but after seeing her today ...

Loki whined and Harley transferred his rub to the dog's ears. 'Don't know how we're going to wriggle out of this one, boy.'

Loki barked and scratched at the floor. He ran to the window and back again.

Harley frowned. 'What's up, boy? Need to pee? Jeez, didn't you pee enough when we were tossing the rope around? You pissed up against every bloody tree on the property twice over, but I guess we can take a walk before I warm us up some dinner. Pity we couldn't talk Tikki into that burger, hey?'

Loki ran out through the door of the study, alternately barking and whining. Harley lifted his jacket from the peg, pulled it on and threw open the front door. The dog tore off across the field heading straight for the gate onto the Chalmers' property.

The smell of smoke hit Harley first followed by the sight of an orange glow that didn't belong to the remnants of the sunset that lit the sky. Thick black smoke rolled out from the roof of the Chalmers homestead, fingers of flames starting to creep up over the old iron panels.

And Jesus, the wind had picked up to blustery sending those suckers flaring all over the place.

'Fuck!'

Thanking his great grandfather's foresight for building the house on Bakers Hill close to the homestead on Golden Acres so they could share a view of the dam, he pulled his mobile phone out of his pocket and dialled triple zero as he ran for the shed. Jesus, if they weren't within sight of each other, he'd never have seen the flames.

When the call centre answered, he gave directions for fire and ambulance as he kick-started his bike with the phone between his ear and elbow.

Panic seized him as he raced after Loki, relieved he hadn't had time to weld the gate shut between their properties and it stood open now, allowing him quick access to the Chalmers' field.

Emergency services were at least twenty minutes away. He had no choice but to do what he could alone. He took the shortest route to the dam pump, switched the sequence to garden irrigation and set it going with a whack on the button. The sprinklers sprang to life erratically on the dry, overgrown bush garden that surrounded the Chalmers' homestead. Fear mixed with the panic raging through his system. Every second counted.

If it did little to save the house, the pump would fill the spare water tank for the firies to use when they got there. In the meantime, it would keep the dry brush around the walls from catching alight and spreading the fire.

Harley geared up across the field, searching for signs of life outside the house. Nothing. The flames had taken hold at the rear right-hand side of the house. The kitchen and mudroom end. Killing the engine, he dropped his bike and ran around the side to turn off the gas supply.

The heat off the side wall sent steam rising as the water from the sprinklers made contact. Damn the old bugger for being such a tight arse and not installing fire suppression systems in his roof like Dad had.

Harley ran back around to the front of the house through the sprinklers, allowing the water to soak his clothes and ignoring the chill the wind sent through his body. Loki bark-howled and pawed at the front door.

'Is there someone in there, boy?'

Loki was the best bloody tracking dog in the world and if he smelled something human, Harley believed him. No time to waste. Where the hell were Tameka and her dad? Terror clawed at his gut as he touched the door handle, the memory of another time, another fire burning in his mind.

Cold. Thank God. The fire hadn't reached beyond the kitchen. Yet. He fought to remember what he knew about backdraft and feeding fire with too much to lose if Tameka was trapped inside the house.

'Stay, Loki.' He pushed open the door. 'Tikki?' Smoke clogged his lungs, and an eerie orange glow filled the dark and gloomy hallway. Heat sucked the air from his chest as he dropped to his knees. 'Mr C!'

Dragging up the memory of the house floor plan, he crawled his way down the hallway to where the smoke billowed through the doorway stinging his eyes. Better check there first where he had the least amount of time. Already his clothes were drying out.

He stood crouched against the heat and covered his mouth with his arm as he headed for the source of the fire. Through the haze of smoke and flicker of flames he saw Tameka near the door, lying on her side. Dead still. Like Ryan. *No.* Outside, Loki howled.

Harley moved fast, dropping to his knees to do a quick assessment of her injuries before hauling her up into his arms and running, the smell of smoke, burning oil and timber following in his wake. He cleared the danger zone and headed for the creek with Loki on his heels, his lungs burning with the effort.

On the grassy bank, he checked her pulse and breathing. Shallow, erratic. Pain squeezed his heart. *Please don't let her die.*

He rolled her onto her side and placed her in the recovery position, her body limp. In the fading light, his stomach clenched at the sight of her burnt shirt. Singed holes where the flames had eaten at the material revealed red raw burns. He'd seen the blisters forming all over her back when he'd found her in the kitchen.

'Tikki, wake up. Where's your dad?'

Tameka moaned, the sound raspy.

'Can you hear me, Tikki?'

With darkness descending quickly as the sun set, he could barely see her face. All he had was the residual light from the fire. Damn, he wished he'd had time to grab a torch.

How long had she been unconscious? He stroked her short hair and ran his fingers over her face, his throat burning from more than smoke inhalation. She stirred and her eyes flickered open.

'Baby, can you hear me?'

'Yeah. Hurts.'

'I know, I know. Ambulance is on the way. Where's your dad?'

She coughed and drew in a short breath. 'Gone.'

'So, he's not in the house?' Harley looked back as the flames roared through the mud room behind the kitchen, well and truly taking hold with the wind up its arse.

'He left.'

'Okay, good. Did you hit your head?'

The glimpse of the blood at her temple before he'd swept her up and run had him worried. Concussion at the very least. Her eyes fluttered closed and a tear leaked down her cheek, but she didn't answer.

'Stay with me, baby.'

God damn it, he wasn't prepared for this to happen again. Too far to carry her to the house and he didn't want to leave her alone to get supplies. And the memories. Jesus, the memories. It *had* happened again.

'I have to get your shirt away from those burns, Tikki, okay? I have to take it off otherwise there's a risk of infection. But only if I can. If it's stuck to your skin, I can't. I'll cover you with my jacket, so you don't get cold.'

Keep talking. Walk her through it. Don't think. Don't think about Ryan, also burnt, also with a head injury.

Ryan — his big brother, his hero. Burnt. Dead. Gone forever. For God's sake, he couldn't lose Tikki too. His chest tightened forcing out a hacking cough.

Harley slipped off his jacket and shivered against the cut of the wind. Carefully, he peeled away Tameka's shirt, checking her skin for burns as he went. Only her back, not her hands, and only a little. A few second, maybe third-degree burns.

He sucked in a breath of relief and ended up coughing smoke from his lungs. No bra. A lifesaver. Polyester crap that would have melted to her skin. He dropped her shirt on the ground and picked up his jacket, throwing it over her. His ears strained to catch the sounds of sirens, his eyes searched for Louis Chalmers, and pain gripped his chest. He didn't want to lose someone he loved to fire again.

Chapter Seven

Tameka shivered under the warmth of Harley's jacket. Her head throbbed and her lungs burned from the smoke. Thoughts churned in her mind. Dad had left her to die. Where was he now?

Her fingers curled around Harley's, torn between telling him and protecting her father who didn't deserve to be protected. Clinging to hope that somewhere inside him there was still a little good because he was the only parent she had left.

The fleeting memories of the father who had done nice things once or twice, a long time ago when she was little and he wasn't drunk all the time, only sometimes. But if she dobbed …

Her thoughts muddled as a wave of pain reverberated through her head and darkness hovered at the edge of her consciousness.

Another day. Another fire. Ryan playing in the shed. Her father's roar of laughter. What she'd seen from behind the tree. The dark memory of a young child resurfacing, regenerating then flitting away on a stab of pain. She moaned against it.

Harley's fingers squeezed hers. 'It's okay, Tikki. You'll be okay.'

Her eyelids flickered. In the distance, embers shot into the sky as the roof over the mudroom caved into the flames. Dad would blame her. Tell the investigators it was her fault, her lousy cooking skills, her clumsiness that had started the fire.

'Help will be here soon.'

She wanted to tell him to go, to save the homestead, fight the fire as best he could with the garden hose. But she couldn't let go of his hand and the warmth of his body close to hers as he shielded her from the bite of the wind and bad memories.

The press of his lips against her knuckles had her eyes fluttering closed. Soft, reassuring. If he knew of the suppressed memory that had surfaced lying there in the burning kitchen, he'd hate her. There'd be more than just the Big Bang to come between them. And now, today, she'd almost died the same way Ryan had.

Harley dropped her hand and she felt him shuffle about before she heard his voice, urgent and full of fear, on the phone to the captain of Wongan Creek's Rural Fire Service.

'For God's sake, Barry, hurry up with the fire trucks or there'll be nothing left. And can you get onto the paramedics too, we need that ambulance now. She's in shock and floating in and out of consciousness. She has a head injury.'

Black edged around her vision, dulling the flicker from the flames. Harley should have left her in the house. Left her to die. She didn't deserve him or his care. Living the way she had for the last eight years … closing her eyes to the wrongs … burying her head in the sand … hoping things would change …

Harley's voice faded from her mind along with the flicker of light and roar of flames into silence.

Sirens. Bright lights. Voices. Harley's hand torn from hers. Bone-jarring movement that made her head thump and her back burn. Soothing cool against her heated skin. The prick of a needle against the back of her hand.

'I'm sorry, love, this might sting a little.'

Soft hands smoothed the frown from her forehead, easing the throb that beat like a drum. A quiet female voice uttered reassuring words as the skin on her hand burned with a jab, then seconds later a small sting and a rush as fluid joined the blood in her veins.

'Harley —'

The nurse patted her hand as she plastered strips over the needle onto the skin of Tameka's hand. 'The doctor is giving him a check over too, and then he'll wait outside to see you. As soon as we've got you sorted, we'll let him in, okay?'

'My head hurts.'

'That's quite a whack you took. Do you remember how that happened?'

How could she forget? But to speak out against her father … maybe it was an accident. Maybe he hadn't meant to hurt her. Just like he hadn't meant to hurt Ryan. Could she trust that memory? What if she'd made it up in her head?

'Fell against the cooktop.'

'That must have hurt. Did you slip on something?'

'Spilled oil.'

The hands soothing her forehead hesitated. A different voice, vaguely familiar as it registered between the drumbeats in her head. 'And your arm, Tameka? How did you get that bruise?'

'Don't know.' Lies. How many more lies would she tell until this was over? Would it ever be over? She moaned as pain clutched her head, smothering the sting of the burns on her back.

'Okay, honey, the pain medication will kick in soon and you'll start to feel better. Who was with you in the house when you fell? Was Harley there?'

'*No.*'

'Do you know where your dad is, honey? Was he hurt in the fire?'

Tameka felt her eyes sting and emotion clog her

throat. She focused on the cold, heady sensation of the oxygen being fed from the tube in through her nose. 'Don't know.' How could she tell them he'd left her alone to burn?

She caught the look the one nurse sent the other and closed her eyes to it. Pity, doubt, questions. There'd be a lot of all three. Later.

The pain in her head began to ease as the questions stopped and the nurses focused on tending her burns and taping the split skin together on her temple. Their voices faded to murmurs as Tameka drifted, not allowing her thoughts to travel down dark roads.

Instead, she focused on the memory of Harley's face, the feel of Loki's short fur body tucked into hers as the dog had warmed her down by the river and didn't think about what would happen when Dad came back to the farm and found she'd survived.

When she woke next, she was in the ward propped up on her side to keep the weight off her back and Harley sitting in a chair right next to the bed with his hands between his knees and his head bent.

'Hey.' The word rasped from her smoke-dry throat.

Harley raised his head. 'Hey. How are you feeling?'

She let a smile spread her lips even though it hurt. Her face felt tight and tender like she'd spent the day out in the field under the sun without a hat. She could still smell the smoke clinging to her skin. 'Sore.'

He straightened his back and unclenched his hands.

'Even your hair is singed.' He ran a hand over her head, his fingers brushing lightly around the bandage on her temple before he let it rest next to her on the sheets, curling his pinkie finger around hers. 'You scared the crap out of me.'

'Where's Loki?' Thinking about what could have happened and what her dad had done only made the ache inside her heart worse.

Harley frowned. He'd know she was being evasive. He knew too much about her. She wanted the fun times back, the easy banter they'd shared throughout their childhood. But that had been taken by Ryan's death, what they'd done — what she'd done — and her mum walking away.

He took a breath and blew it out. 'Mum and Dad picked him up a while ago. They've taken him home with them.' He smiled and her heart skipped a beat. 'The ambos let him ride with me. He wanted to get into the ambulance with you, but they were worried about infection. I think my dog has a crush on you.'

'He is kinda sweet … when he's not ploughing up my fields.' She coughed as her lungs burned still with the effort to breathe, the sound harsh in the almost empty ward. 'Are you okay?'

'Better than you. My throat's a little sore from the smoke. A bit of heat rash from the flames.'

'I'm sorry, Harley. You could have died in there … looking for me.'

'I would have lost another part of myself if I wasn't in time to save you, Tikki. Jesus, minutes later and —'

And he might have been too late. She'd be gone, just like Ryan. She held that intense gaze for a long moment, let it warm the ice in her heart and ease the lead weight in her stomach. Was he thinking of his brother too? 'How much is left?'

Harley shrugged, the movement heavy on his shoulders. 'They were still fighting the fire when we left. The whole kitchen, the mudroom and laundry — all gone. What's left will have smoke and water damage. You won't be able to live there for a while.'

So much for her dreams for the homestead. Had Dad even paid the insurance premiums lately? She didn't have a clue what state their finances were in. Dad kept the files under lock and key. He managed the finances, she managed the physical workload. Would he come back and report the incident to the insurance company, or would he stay away, shake the humiliation of Golden Acres from his boots?

'Was the ute outside the house?'

Harley shook his head. 'I don't remember seeing it. Do you think your dad took it? Do you know where he went?'

Questions. Too many questions. 'I'm tired. So tired. Go home. I'll be fine.'

Harley sighed and loosened his pinkie from around

hers. 'When will you let me back in, Tikki? Let me take care of you while we sort this out.'

She closed her eyes, shutting out the hard-to-resist offer in his words. It would be so easy to let him in. But then the horror of the last eight years would unfold, and the town would know what her father was really like. And she'd be judged by his measure using the same yardstick, just as they had in the hardware store.

She'd have to face more questions, more pitying looks, and live with a scandal that small town gossip would grow by adding to the story through speculation. Like a picture painted with many hands and different artistic interpretation.

'Later.' She listened to the sound of his chair scraping back as he stood, felt the mattress dip under his weight and the press of his lips to her cheek.

'Would you like me to keep an eye out on the farm while you're here?'

'Okay, thanks.'

'You can stay in my spare room until you get things sorted.'

'I can stay at the caravan park.'

Harley sighed. 'Whatever you think is best, but at least you can keep an eye out over your place if you stay at mine. No strings attached.'

'I'll think about it, thanks.' She hated this awkwardness between them and the reasons her tongue couldn't form the words when her heart screamed 'yes'.

His hand touched her shoulder, his fingers squeezing reassuringly, before his palm trailed down her arm. She flinched as it skimmed over the tender spot where her dad had gripped her forearm.

Harley pulled his hand away. 'That's a nasty bruise, Tikki.'

She evened her breathing and faked sleep until his footsteps faded from the room.

Chapter Eight

Watery sunshine filtered in through the window on the ward, the beams catching the fine sprinkles of dust in the air. Tameka let her gaze fall on the empty seat where Harley had sat the night before.

She was glad there was no-one else in the room, grateful for the silence. In silence, she could think, plan. Another chance to leave, to shake the soil of Wongan Creek from her boots. When they handed her the discharge form, she'd be free. And with Dad gone, it would be so easy to take the first bus out of town.

Tentacles of doubt and fear of the unknown wrapped themselves around the thought. At least on Golden Acres, she knew what she was dealing with, had learnt to read Dad's moods—when to hide, when to stay, when to keep quiet.

She knew the land and how to work it, the trials, and challenges. To leave and look for work in another town with no references, work among strangers after living with the familiar all her life, take the risk that Dad might come looking for her. Or not. To leave Harley forever or wait until she was free to find him again. How long would he wait for her before he gave up?

'Tameka?'

She turned her head to see a man wearing the navy-blue Rural Fire Service uniform and epaulettes that gave him rank.

'Yes?'

'Barry Metcalfe, captain of Wongan Creek's Rural Fire Service. How are you doing? A little better than last night, I hope?'

Here came the questions. Some she could answer, others she wouldn't. Not to protect her father, but to protect herself. 'Yes, thank you.'

'Good.' Barry blew out a breath. 'Right. I realise this might be a difficult time for you, but I have to ask you some questions.'

'Sure, go ahead.' Tameka tried to keep the resignation from her tone. She'd been expecting them all while wishing she could avoid them.

'Whenever there are injuries sustained in a fire, we are required to file a report. This helps us to identify the various causes of house fires and allows us to develop better training and prevention measures.' He walked around the bed so he could face her, pulled the chair a little closer and sat.

'I understand.' She'd tell him what she could, keep the emotion out of it and stick to the facts, even if she had to omit a few.

The captain of Wongan Creek's Rural Fire Service was the kind of man she felt she could trust. The vibe he gave out put her at ease. At the very least, his presence was far from intimidating. He made her feel safe — a true hero, a protector and, if she remembered correctly, a father himself.

He'd be a good dad, a kind one who'd discipline his children without violence but with a firm hand that requested respect rather than demanded it.

'Good, makes my job a whole lot easier.' His smile was easy and friendly, reassuring. 'If there is any suspicion of criminal intent, we have to report it to the police. So, for example, if the fire was deliberately lit that would be arson.'

She liked his gentle smile, the kindness and empathy in his expression, the quiet way he spoke. If only her dad could be more like Barry Metcalfe.

'I understand. The fire was an accident. It was my fault. I knocked the bottle of oil onto the flames.'

The truth, perhaps not the whole truth, but an investigation into how the fire started would uncover more questions than she wanted to give answers to. All she wanted was for everything — the fire, her father, the last miserable few years — to go away.

Barry frowned at her quick admission, but nodded after a moment, accepting her explanation. 'I understand. We aren't investigating that it was deliberately lit. We could see the source of ignition. You had a lucky escape.'

Luck depended on which point of view he was looking at it from. Tameka closed her eyes against the thought. Lucky to be alive, lucky to not have sustained worse injuries. Unlucky not to have escaped the cycle she found herself in. Unable to leave, reluctant to stay. She let the tears that stung her eyes fall before dashing them away. She'd cheated death, and there had to be a damn good reason for that even if she had no idea what it was yet.

Chief Metcalfe handed her a tissue from the box on the metal cabinet next to the bed. 'We also understand that fires can be devastating for victims particularly those who have sustained injuries. We can direct you to counselling services if you need them. It's not unusual for victims to suffer from post-traumatic stress disorder following injury or loss from fire.'

'Thank you, I'll keep that in mind.'

He smiled and consulted his clipboard. 'Good, because I've asked Heather Bailey to come in and introduce herself to you in case you'd like to make use of her services. Right, let's get these questions out the way then, shall we? I'm sure you'd like to get some more rest.'

What she wanted was out, away from the questions, the speculation. She didn't want counselling either, but refusing now would only raise more questions. Maybe answering Captain Metcalfe's questions would stop other people from asking, so she answered them as he ticked them off on his list.

'Now, I understand your dad wasn't in the house, is that right?'

Tameka nodded. 'He came in while I was cooking dinner, but it wasn't ready yet, so he left.' And still, she was protecting him. Why couldn't she tell the captain the truth?

He stepped over me on his way out the door instead of reaching for the fire blanket.

'Okay, were you expecting him to come back?'

No, he didn't even look back. 'I had no reason to think he wouldn't.' *Liar.*

'Right, because we were there until late mopping up and a crew went out there to finish up this morning, but there was still no sign of your father. We'll need to talk to him too since he's the owner of the property. Any idea where he went or when he'll be back?'

At last, a question she could answer honestly. 'I don't know.'

Footsteps echoed over the hard floor and Barry looked up with a smile.

'Heather, hi. Thank you for coming in.'

'Hi, Barry. No problem at all. I'm on a mission from the CWA anyway.'

Barry grinned. 'Didn't think it would take long for them to gather the troops.'

'They've been gathered all week on some crisis or another. Things in town are a little hectic at the moment.' Heather stepped around the bed to stand next to Barry. 'Hi, Tameka, I'm Heather, Travis Bailey's wife. We haven't had a chance to meet yet. The ladies asked me to come around and see if there was anything you might need. Clothes, supplies, that sort of thing.' She squeezed Tameka's hand gently. 'I'm so sorry to hear about your accident.'

'Thank you.' Tameka shivered. Everyone would be sorry, most of their regret genuine until they found out the truth and then they'd turn on her, shut her out. The well-meaning comfort would turn to gossipy spite on which the thorns would grow bigger every time it was shared around.

Barry stood. 'Sit, Heather. I'm about to leave anyway. Tameka, thank you for answering those questions. I doubt we'll need to file a police report given that it was an accident, but I'll let you know for sure, okay?'

'No problem, thanks.' Relief flooded her. If they didn't ask any further questions about it, they wouldn't poke at her father when … if … he returned.

'Good, good. Now get some rest and follow the doctor's orders. We want to see you up and about again soon. Please call me if you have any questions or need anything, okay? Are you all right for somewhere to stay when you're discharged?'

She thought of Harley's offer which she hadn't accepted or rejected yet. 'I am. If not, I'll rent a cabin or van at the caravan park.' Even though she had no idea how she would pay for it with the balance of her allowance teetering on the edge of zero.

'Excellent.' He put his card beside the tissue box. 'My contact details in case you need them.' With a wave, he left.

'Such a nice man,' murmured Heather.

Tameka forced a smile to her lips even though they quivered. 'Yes, he is.'

The hard shell she'd grown around her heart had so many cracks in it now that she'd need a barrel of super glue to fix it before the people of Wongan Creek found a way to crumble it completely.

Heather pulled the chair Barry had vacated closer and sat. 'I hope you don't mind me popping in? I guess Barry explained it all from a professional point of view?'

'I don't mind.' Not exactly the truth. She did mind, but Heather seemed like a nice girl. 'It's very kind of you to visit.'

Tameka gave her a wavering smile. What she really

wanted was solitude, but Heather's presence brought a subtle soothing with it that settled her nerves. She liked the gentle smile that curved her mouth, the kindness she saw in Heather's warm brown eyes, and the laughter lines that fanned out from the edges onto flawless, creamy skin that hinted at her Irish heritage.

Tameka tried to remember what she knew about Heather Bailey. Fairly new in town, Harry's missing granddaughter, a social worker. Her heart skipped a beat. Someone like Heather was trained to read the signs. She'd see the bruises and wonder, ask a barrage of questions. If she did the math, would she come up with the right answer? Dear God, she hoped not. Explanations would result in an organised search for her father, the whole situation would escalate out of control, and she'd be the one to pay the price when he talked his way out of it.

Barry and the ladies at the CWA had meant well sending Heather here, their actions kind and generous. It wasn't their fault she wasn't used to being treated with care, it was hers, but she had to keep her guard up around Heather Bailey.

Heather leaned forward, her hands resting on the edge of the bed. 'Tameka, I'm not here in an official capacity only. Travis and Harley have been friends for a long time. I hope we can be too. It's tough being the new girl in town and I'm still feeling my way around, making friends as I go. I won't press you or ask questions you don't want to answer, but I'd like you to know that you can trust me if you need to talk through what happened.'

Tameka felt the prick of tears again. She hadn't cried this much since Mum left. She had to get a handle on it because tears signified weakness and weak was something she couldn't afford to be.

'Thank you, I appreciate that.'

'Good.' Heather reached down into her handbag and pulled out a diary. 'Let's make that list, shall we? Oh, before I forget, Casey asked me to give you this.' She unfolded a piece of A4 paper she'd pulled from between the pages. 'She drew it for you.'

'Casey? Travis' niece?' Tameka remembered the little girl, orphaned as a toddler when her mother drowned in the creek.

She reached for the picture, wincing as the movement stretched her tender skin. On the page, a blue butterfly flew towards the sun over a green paddock dotted with woolly sheep. The words *get well soon*, formed with the shaky hand of a child learning to write, curved around the sun. In the bottom corner, Casey had signed her name and written the date. 'That's beautiful. Please tell her I said thank you.'

'Would you like me to ask the nurse to put it up on the wall for you?'

Alone in the ward, there were no cheerful bouquets and get well soon cards around for other patients to brighten up the otherwise clinical space. 'That would be lovely, thank you.'

Heather opened the diary to a blank page and placed her pen in the groove of the spine. 'I'm surprised they didn't send you to Perth for treatment.'

Strangers, more questions, and the frightening thought that those questions would lead to further investigations. As if she wasn't afraid enough of what would happen when her father came back. If he came back. 'I'm glad they didn't. Luckily, the emergency department here has been upgraded to handle burns cases. One of the advantages the gold mine has brought to the town.'

'That and John's guilty conscience that encouraged a healthy donation for the new equipment.' Heather grinned. 'It's about time that man dug into those deep pockets of his instead of trying to make money out of the townsfolk by snapping up properties, either prospecting or subdividing them.'

Tameka relaxed a little as the conversation moved from her situation to more general topics and eventually to the list of things she'd need to tide her over while she was in hospital. By the time Heather dropped her diary back into her bag and searched out her keys, Tameka felt she really had gained a new friend.

But what value did that friendship have if, when her father returned, she'd have to withdraw again? Go back to being the person she had to be to protect the people she cared about from his wild mood swings and erratic behaviour. The way she hadn't been able to protect her mother. The way she'd had to let go to protect Harley.

Harley. Damn him for making her want things again she couldn't afford to keep. Like peace, love and stability, and a safe place to be the person she wanted to be.

Chapter Nine

The days had run on into each other leaving him exhausted — emotionally, physically, and mentally. Harley's dreams had turned to nightmares haunted by faces that alternated between Ryan's and Tameka's. The smell of smoke clung stubbornly to his skin despite scrubbing it away, like the guilt that clung to his heart and mind. If he'd done things differently, if he hadn't screwed up, Ryan would be alive today to give him shit and Tameka wouldn't be lying injured in a hospital bed.

He'd worked from sparrow's fart in the morning until long after the sun had set in the evening so he'd be too tired to dream while he worried about Tameka and what would happen next. Would she accept his offer or stubbornly proceed with her plan to rent a cabin at the caravan park?

He'd spent five long days of alternating between his farm and Tikki's, visiting the hospital every day, keeping an eye out for the return of her old man, praying Chalmers would stay away and Tameka would come home to Bakers Hill so he could make it up to her somehow.

A taxi pulled into Harley's driveway and Tameka got out. She still hadn't agreed to stay with him, and he'd left her to make up her own mind.

Harley put his empty plate down on the wooden slats of the veranda floor and let Loki lick it clean. He watched and listened to the minor argument as the driver refused to take payment for the ride and smiled. The ride from town out to Bakers Hill would be worth at least a hundred bucks. Cash Jeremy Little couldn't really afford to lose with five kids to feed and his wife pregnant with the sixth. He'd make sure Mum dropped off a food parcel at the Little house as thank you for the man's kindness.

Tameka waved Jeremy away and turned to walk up the steps, the overnight bag Harley had loaned her in her hands. She stopped on the top step and looked at Loki, her eyebrows raised, a sight for sore eyes in a flannel shirt too big for her and trackpants too loose with the waistband riding her hips.

Harley ignored the stutter of his heart and shrugged. 'What? I'm putting the dishes through the rinse cycle.'

'With dog slobber?' She put the bag down gingerly, a wince drawing her mouth tight.

'Loki's mouth is a hell of a lot cleaner than some people I know.'

'No argument there.'

'How's the head?'

'Better.' She touched her fingers to the white medical tape covering the wound. 'Throb's gone.'

'And your back?' Harley picked up the plate Loki had licked clean. 'See? Spotless. Don't even need to wash it. I could put it right back in the cupboard and no-one would know the difference.'

She grinned and his heart almost stopped beating altogether. 'You're an idiot. My back is okay. The skin is tight, but the lesser burns have started to heal. The doctor says I need someone to apply ointment on them three times a day. Think you can handle that?'

He could if his hands stopped shaking and his mind didn't remember what her body felt like under his palms. 'The caravan park residents couldn't handle it, hey?' he teased.

Loki wandered over and lolled against her leg. *Traitor.* She leaned down to scratch behind his ears. Harley snorted at the dumb look of satisfaction on his meant-to-be-ferocious watchdog's face.

'They're all too busy planning the next leg of their road trip.' She patted Loki's head and the dog nudged at her hand for more.

He never thought he'd be jealous of his dog. Harley stepped forward and picked up the overnight bag, trying to suppress the hope that flared in his heart. He couldn't afford to read any more into this than it was — Tameka needing a place to stay. 'Righto. Spare room's made up, sheets are clean, and there are a couple of towels and some toiletries in the en suite. Let me know what else you need, and I'll get Mum to pick it up.'

She transferred her hand from Loki's head to Harley's arm. 'Thanks.'

He lifted his free hand to touch her face. 'You're welcome.' And because he wanted to kiss her and let her know how happy he was that she was alive, okay, and right where he needed her to be, he let her go. 'I'll put this in your room and then we'll take a walk over to your place. I'm sure you'll want to see the damage. Captain Metcalfe has given clearance as safe to enter. We can go into the front rooms and bedrooms, but whatever's left of the back of the house will need to be torn down so it's off limits. They've stabilised it with steel props and scaffolding at the damaged end.'

He didn't add that the sight and smell of the burnt-out homestead had raised memories of Ryan, haunting him with recollections like the fishing rod his brother would never pick up again and the pain of watching his hero lowered into the ground in a wooden box that shouldn't have been so damn small.

'Yeah, thanks. I'd like to see what I can salvage, especially clothing-wise. Heather and I made a list, and the CWA ladies brought me some second-hand stuff. Loose is good right now.' She tugged at the tail of the oversize shirt.

'I might have to lend you a couple of mine then. I'm not sure we'll get the smoke smell out of what's left over there. Loki's talents only run to cleaning dishes.'

Tameka punched his arm. 'You know all you need to do is pick up the phone and you'll have half a dozen women out here with washing powder and fabric softener ready to do your laundry.'

The only laundry he wanted doing was his and Tameka's. Together. Forever. But it was too soon to hope that this was the first step towards renewing what they never should have lost.

'I'm a twenty-first-century man. I can turn a knob on a washing machine.' He could press buttons too, but she wasn't ready for that yet.

'Can you still make a cup of tea?' She eyed him hopefully.

'You bet. I've got some leftover barbecue chicken if you want a roll.'

'Sounds like heaven. I swear they're still using powdered eggs in the hospital kitchen. Crazy when we've got so many chooks running around the place.'

He waved her ahead of him through the front door

and watched her slow and painful progress down the hallway to the guest bedroom. 'When do you need that ointment applied?'

'While I'm waiting for my tea to cool down and my chicken roll to digest with my painkillers.'

He wanted to stop her, turn her around and hold her close to make her pain go away. 'Great. I'll get right onto that, Princess Tameka.'

'Good. And the dog stays with me.'

'You're kidnapping my dog?'

'Just for a little while. I need a cuddle.'

'Mine aren't good enough?'

She took the bag from his hand, stepped into the room with the dog and turned around to face him. 'They're too good and it's been a long time since the last one. I'm not ready for them yet.' The door closed gently in his face.

Bloody woman. He held a hand over his heart to keep it in his chest, leaned his forehead against the door and listened to the murmur of her voice as she spoke quietly to Loki. She'd be okay. She *was* okay. He turned away and walked to the kitchen to make her a sandwich and a cup of tea.

He'd barely squeezed out the teabag and put the milk in her tea when Tameka walked into the kitchen. She eyed the chicken mayo roll as he placed the mug next to the plate.

'Looks good. I could eat a horse.'

He pretended not to see the redness around her eyes or the tear tracks on her cheeks when she dropped a tube of ointment and a packet of painkillers on the table. Only the dog knew for sure what those tears were about.

'Maybe I'd better take Loki for a run while you eat then. In case you get any ideas.'

'Funny. You always did think you were a comedian.'

Harley walked around the table and pulled out the chair opposite her, slipping into it. He interlocked his fingers, let his hands rest on the table, watched her eat and said nothing.

Tameka closed her eyes and chewed. 'That's damn good chicken. Did you make it?'

'Annie Hamilton brought it over.' His freezer was full of Wongan Creek bachelorette-made meals, right next to the ones his mother insisted he'd need if Tameka came to stay.

'You should marry that girl.'

'I'm more of a stir fry kinda guy.'

Tameka stopped chewing and looked at him with those beautiful eyes shaped like a lazy cat's, neither brown nor hazel but something in between, the angles of her features softened by the mix of Australian and Asian genes. 'Then you need to change your diet.'

'I tried.'

'Try harder. Me staying here isn't about us, Harley. I'm taking advantage of your hospitality because my field is over the fence, and it makes sense to be closer to home to take care of my livelihood.' She pushed her empty plate away. 'And as much as I love your dog, he's not licking the crumbs off my plate.'

Harley tried hard not to smile and failed. Tikki always got on the defensive when she was in denial. It gave him hope because damn it, he'd never stopped loving her or wanting her back. 'Whatever. Do you want me to put ointment on your back now?'

'That would be great, thanks.'

He stood, washed his hands at the sink and rubbed disinfectant gel over them just in case. She'd been through enough without having to suffer secondary infections that might see her heading to Perth for further treatment. He pulled the first aid kit down from the shelf in the pantry and carried it over to the table then filled a clean, not-washed-by-Loki cereal bowl with warm water.

'Lift your shirt.'

He sucked in his breath as he dampened the bandages with water before peeling them away. While the first-degree burns had started to heal over and the second-degree burns were still raw, pink, and inflamed, it was the third-degree burns with their charred look that made his heart ache. She flinched as he applied ointment to the lesser burns higher up her back with a cotton swab.

'Sorry.'

'It's okay. They're just sensitive.'

'Will they heal completely?'

'In time if I take care of them properly and don't get any infections, but the worst ones will leave puckered skin and nerve damage.' She folded her arms on the table and rested her forehead on them. 'I can't feel those.'

Harley felt the sigh shudder through her. 'Will you need skin grafts?'

'The doctor doesn't think it will be necessary. I have to wear a pressure suit until they've healed. Taking that thing off and putting it back on again is a bitch.'

That would explain some of the tears his dog would have witnessed earlier. No way in hell would she take anything off without feeling pain. And she'd had to take it off so he could apply the ointment.

'You should have called me to help.'

'I managed. I'll need to apply tissue oil once the healing process is complete to repair the scarring. Mum used to use this stuff called silica that boosts collagen. That might help.'

And damn it, he'd buy up the world's supply of it for her if he could just convince the bank to extend his loan and grant him a grace period. 'I'm sorry, baby.'

He applied gauze and bandages to the wounds, pressed a kiss to her bare shoulder and tried not to think about Ryan who hadn't been as lucky to escape a fire. He'd have given the world to see his mother tend his brother's burns instead of having to attend his funeral.

He'd give a lot more to have him here today, alive. That he'd almost lost Tikki the same way …

He drew back and let his fingers travel across her cheek, her skin soft and damp with tears. His own eyes burned as a lump of sadness lodged in his throat.

'Don't.' She lifted her head a little, looking over her shoulder at him. 'Don't feel sorry for me or for what happened to me, Harley. I can deal with this on my own. As I've dealt with everything else.'

Everything else. What had she dealt with alone all the years, for God's sake, besides running the farm? He'd watched her out there alone in the field, her father conspicuous by his absence. The only help she'd had was hired during harvest. Even that had been minimal, outsourced beyond the borders of Wongan Creek because no-one wanted to deal with an arsehole like Louis Chalmers any more than he wanted to deal with them.

He held her gaze, dropped her shirt, turned her around chair and all, and knelt in front of her. He wished things could be different, that he hadn't screwed up that day in the front seat of his ute and dropped her right in the shit with her dad. Hell, he'd dropped them both knee-deep in a pile of it.

'Tikki, I can't change what happened in the past, but I know I love you. I always have. Nothing will change that. No matter how much time and distance you put between us.'

She looked at him in silence, her eyes searching his in a way that had his body stirring and his mind closing the bedroom door. And then they turned sad, and his chest tightened.

'I can never be that person for you, Harley. There is so much …' She lifted a hand to his face and pressed her forehead to his. 'So much.'

'Tell me.'

'I can't. Not yet. Maybe never.'

Loki pushed between them and knocked Harley back on his arse. 'Jesus, Loki.' He ruffled the dog's ears. 'Looks like I'm outnumbered.'

Tameka stood slowly, carefully. 'Your dog is smarter than you. We should go over to the homestead before it gets too dark.'

Harley pushed himself up off the floor. 'I guess so.' He held out his hand and she slipped hers into it, a gesture of friendship rather than intimacy. 'I'm a little concerned that your dad hasn't come back yet. He's been gone for over four days. Did you want me to file a missing person's report?'

Her fingers tightened around his. 'No, he'll come back when he's ready.'

'He's not answering his phone.'

She froze at Harley's side. 'You rang him?'

'Well, I rang the number Dad had for him. It went straight to message bank.'

'Harley!'

'What? Jesus, Tameka, he needs to know his daughter almost died when his house burnt down.'

Harley dragged a hand through his hair. Why the hell was she so angry with him for calling her dad? So, the relationship wasn't great, but he had a duty of care to fulfil.

Her nostrils flared, her throat worked, and her eyes took on a haunted look, and he realised she wasn't angry … she was afraid.

The bruise on her arm after the fire had been finger shaped. Louis Chalmers was an aggressive bastard with a quick temper.

'You don't want your dad to be found, do you?' And there he was, leaping to conclusions again. 'You'd rather he stayed away.'

'It's not like that.'

'The fire wasn't an accident, was it? Where was he that night?'

'The fire was my fault.' Her eyes dropped to the top of Loki's head. She hooked a finger under his collar and the dog leaned closer. 'He went out.'

'Out where?' Harley placed his hands on her shoulders. 'Did he go before or after the fire started, Tameka?'

Her head came back up, her gaze landed somewhere north of his shoulder and her tone was fraught with bitterness. 'Stop with the frigging questions! I don't know, okay?'

With every fibre of his being and beat of his heart, Harley knew Tameka was lying through her pretty white teeth. Or at the very least, not telling the whole truth. Which made him even more certain that Louis Chalmers had something to do with the fire and it scared him shitless.

Chapter Ten

She wanted to tell him. About her dad, the way her mum left, what she thought she saw the day Ryan died and the memories that had resurfaced the night of the fire. Everything. But then Harley would hate her the way she hated herself for being a pawn in her father's cruel, emotionally, and sometimes physically hurtful game.

No-one would understand why she hoped he had gone for good, just as no-one would understand why she couldn't simply pack her bags and leave. How a part of her wished he wouldn't come back. That he would use the gun he loaded every night on himself and not some innocent victim he'd take out in a fit of rage. And then she wouldn't have to live with another innocent death on her conscience. Only her father's — which would be a blessing in the disguise of a tragedy.

But with him dead, she might have even less than she had now. No home, no family, no income, the scandal that would follow … Then she'd have to leave town because, when he knew the truth, the man she loved would abandon her too.

And when the truth hit the news, the town's residents wouldn't simply accept her self-exclusion from the community, they'd turn on her the way Mal and Ahn had in the hardware store that day when she'd needed the seeder hose fixed, only worse.

Harley released her shoulders. 'I'll lend you a coat. The wind has a bite today.'

'Thanks. I have to put my pressure suit back on first.'

'Okay. Do you need help with that?'

'Please.'

She'd like to say no. Getting out of it was one thing, getting back into it with its front-fastening zipper required flexibility she wouldn't have again for a while. Not when every twist or turn stretched the skin around the burns and hurt the lesser ones or made the worst ones on her lower back bleed. But it had been a long time since Harley had seen her in her knickers and nothing else.

'Let's do it then. I don't want you out there in the wind too long.' Harley nudged her in the direction of the guest bedroom.

'Don't baby me, Baker.'

His hands went to his hips, and he dipped his head to stare at the floor. He let out a long breath edged with something she couldn't quite put her finger on. Annoyance? Irritation? Resignation?

'I wouldn't dare.'

Smart-arse. She turned and walked down the hallway to her room. Inside she picked up the pressure suit from the bed where she'd left it after cuddling Loki and crying her frustration into his short, brindled fur. A moment of weakness she wouldn't let happen again. She held up the suit and Harley took it from her.

'Looks like a shortie wetsuit.' He twisted it in his hands before drawing the zipper down. 'Very sexy. You could kick off a whole new trend in underwear in this town.'

'Very funny.'

Tameka unbuttoned her shirt. She hesitated with her fingers hooked into the waistband of her trackpants. Once the drawstring was loosened, they should drop right off. And when she shrugged off her shirt, she'd be totally exposed. Not just her back which he'd already seen, but her breasts which had matured since he'd seen them last, the contours of her body that were all muscle and no fat thanks to physical labour, and the hideous underwear donated to charity that the CWA ladies had so kindly brought in for her.

Completely naked with a man who'd once known every inch of her body intimately, but now knew nothing of what clouded her mind and stopped her from walking into his arms and feeling whole again. He was looking at her, waiting. She could feel his gaze on her face as she avoided looking into his eyes.

'I'd ask if you need help undressing, but since you're so determined to be Miss Independence …' He tipped up her chin and she let her gaze drift to his. 'Bugger it, let me help you. Like it or slap me. Here, hold your sexy lingerie.'

She clenched the pressure suit in a barrier between them as his fingers hooked under the collar of the shirt and eased it down over her shoulders. Even with the small distance between their bodies, she felt the welcoming heat of his as the material slipped away. He leaned a little closer to toss the shirt onto the bed behind her, his hand still on her shoulder.

Tameka wanted to lean her head against his chest, breathe in the reality and stability that was and always had been Harley. But that would be a weakness, another crack in the wall she'd built and if she did, she'd prove her father right that she was nothing more than a useless female who could never cut it in life without a man.

'Ready for the trackies to come off?'

His hands were warm on her hips, a light and gentle touch as she stared at his chest and tried to ignore the lure of the haven his body promised. She lifted her hands to his shoulders for balance, still clutching the suit between them, as he loosened the drawstring and pushed the pants down over her hips. The material slipped to the floor and pooled at her ankles. She stepped out of them and kicked them back out of the way as she watched Harley's throat work and his gaze focus on something over her shoulder.

Tameka dropped her hands and toyed with the stretchy fabric of the suit. 'Thanks.'

'Yeah.' He took the suit from her. 'How does this thing work?'

'Like a onesie.'

'Right.' He drawled the word as he went down on his knees and held it out. 'Step in.'

She placed her hands on his shoulders again, all too aware that his cheek was close to the hideous orange and pink-striped cotton briefs a size too big. And the heat she was feeling by having him there had nothing to do with embarrassment over undies she would never have chosen for herself.

She stepped into the suit, and he pulled it up over her legs, his hands brushing her thighs and making her breath hitch. His face so close to her abdomen, a place he used to press his lips to create ripples of excitement and desperate desire. But no more, not ever again.

He let the suit hang from her hips and her hands drop from his shoulders as he stood. 'Okay so far?'

Way too close and not okay at all because she wanted him to wrap his arms around her and hold on tight.

Tameka closed her eyes and nodded. Now came the tricky part. The part that hurt in some places and not in others. Places she'd likely never feel sensation again. Unlike the heated sensations Harley's nearness was causing.

'From behind?' His voice was soft and throaty near her ear, drawing her into his warmth.

'Hmmm?' With his hands skimming her body and him all around her, the words took on a whole new meaning and created a vision of another time and place when her back wasn't burnt, and her emotions weren't as scarred.

He chuckled and pressed a kiss to her forehead. 'Is it better if I help you into the suit from behind you or from in front of you?'.'

Heat flushed her cheeks. *Get a grip, girl!* She leaned into him a little longer. 'From the back.'

'Good, because looking at your front is a little distracting and you're in no shape for what's going through my mind right now.'

Tameka rolled her eyes and drew on the line-up of acerbic comebacks she'd accumulated to protect herself with. If he knew her mind had headed in the same direction as his, they'd both be in trouble.

'You're such a guy. Anyone would swear you've never seen boobs before.'

'Oh, I've seen boobs before, baby. Plenty of them whether I wanted to or not. But there's only one pair that mean a damn thing to me. Now turn around so we can get this thing on you to cover them up.' Hands on her hips, he turned her around. 'Pick an arm to go in first.'

She leaned forward a little, wincing as she held out her right arm first — the side with the most damage. Harley's fingers circled her wrist, and he eased her arm through the hole then did the same with the left before settling the suit over her shoulders.

She turned back to face him, fingers on the tab of the zipper. 'I've got it from here.'

'Oh, hell no, this is the best part.' He pushed her hands away and drew it up slowly, his knuckles brushing her skin, sending little shivers skittering through her blood.

'Harley …' She covered his hand with hers, wanting him to stop, making him keep going, needing more than she could have.

'Shh.' He covered her mouth with his and kissed her until her knees buckled, the zipper reached the end of its journey, and her hands were trapped between them. 'I'm glad you're alive, Tikki.' He whispered the words against her ear before delivering a soft tap on her backside with the flat of his hand. 'Now get some clothes on before I change my mind.'

He stepped away, picked up her trackpants and held them out. She took them, sat down on the bed, and pulled them on while he retrieved her discarded shirt. She couldn't let him back into her heart because that heart was a stone and the lies and secrets stored in her mind would turn his own heart hard when he found out.

He might be glad she was alive, but it might have been better for everyone if she *had* died in that fire. Then the truth she wasn't sure was even real would have died with her. And the only person who knew the truth was a bitter, angry, unstable man who'd tried to kill his own daughter.

Now was the time to escape. To run as far away from Wongan Creek as she could while Dad was gone. But like Mum, she'd be leaving with nothing but secrets and no future anywhere. *If you run, Tameka, your mother will never find you.* And so, she'd stay. In case, one day, Mum came looking for her.

'Ready to raid what's left of the homestead?' Harley's voice edged into her thoughts.

'I guess.'

'Get a wriggle on then, princess. Loki's getting impatient.'

Tameka smiled as Loki raced out of the room and back in again, barking with excitement. She let Harley help her into the shirt and slip her boots on, her eyes on his head as he did up the laces, her fingers itching to run through his hair and bring his lips back to hers so she could forget.

He stood, held out his hand and she took it, his warmth and strength enveloping her. She could do this. She could face the almost empty homestead with its meagre furnishings and unhappy memories. She would stay and face her father's return, bear the consequences if he didn't. One foot in front of the other, one step at a time. Alone. As soon as she could bring herself to let go of Harley's hand.

Chapter Eleven

The afternoon sun did little to take the chill off the wind as Harley and Tameka made their way across the fields to the homestead with Loki between them. It sparkled on the surface of the dam and Harley remembered the summers when they were kids — him, Ryan, and Tameka — cooling off in the water before old man Chalmers would chase them out.

Down closer to the river, the homestead stood charred at one end with a bright yellow tarp covering the open roof space where walls had crumbled, and the rafters collapsed. Tameka reached for his hand, and he let his fingers curl around hers as he looked for signs that her dad had returned. The battered white ute he normally parked in the open shed away from the house was still nowhere to be seen.

A memory edged its way into Harley's thoughts of the shed that had stood there before. The one where Ryan had died in a vicious fire that had trapped him inside with no way to escape, a ten-year-old boy who'd been playing with matches on someone else's property. An accident that had gone horribly wrong in a shed full of flammable fertilisers and fuel.

The same compounds Chalmers insisted on using today that had led to half of Harley's crop being destroyed. Now another fire on the Chalmers property and another life that could have been taken in the worst possible way.

He tried to bury the anger that surged for Tameka's sake. This wasn't her fault even though she'd said it was. That she'd started the fire by knocking over the bottle of oil onto the open flame of the gas cooktop. It didn't make sense. If she had, her front would be burnt not her back. Why had she had her back to the flames?

It wasn't to reach for the fire extinguisher. That was on the wall right next to the cooktop. That and the fire blanket. He remembered Mai Chalmers insisting on it, had watched them being installed right after the fire that had destroyed the shed and taken Ryan's life.

Yet according to the fire investigators, neither had been used. Barry Metcalfe had reached the conclusion that Tameka had been alone in the kitchen and hadn't had time to reach for either of the tools that could have saved her from the burns she'd received. She hadn't denied it.

If it wasn't for Loki alerting him to the fire that night … God, he didn't want to think about what the outcome could have been.

He didn't want to ask too many questions either. Not yet. Not until Tameka opened up to him again. She could be as stubborn as a bloody mule if she didn't want to talk. She always had been.

The eight years she'd stayed away from him proved that. Any meetings had been by chance, and she'd said little or nothing when they had. Other than a wave of greeting across the fence, she'd kept her distance. And every time she did, hope for rekindling their friendship if nothing else, had died.

Loki took off after a flock of cockatoos and Tameka edged closer to Harley as the smell of the burnt house drifted towards them in the wind. The tarp billowed and sank back down again as a gust blew through the gaps of what used to be windows but were now nothing more than shattered glass and empty frames.

'We don't have to go inside, Tikki.' Harley stopped walking. 'We can find stuff at my place for you to wear.'

He hoped she'd agree because damn it, the bloody place looked forsaken and miserable against the backdrop of the creek. He shivered, cold from everything including the wind.

'No, I have to do this. At least the office was at the other end of the house. Hopefully, I'll be able to find insurance papers and whatever else I'll need in there. Have everything ready in case … for when Dad comes back.' She tugged on his hand. 'Come on. No point wasting time.'

She was strong, determined and hurting inside. Her defence against emotion had always been to act. Doing was the equivalent of hiding. Harley wished she would let go like she had that day in the ute when she'd been all woman and want. When she'd let him take care of her and love her the way they'd both wanted. Until her father had slammed the door on any dreams of a future.

'It can wait, Tikki.'

'No, it can't.' She dropped his hand and turned to face him. 'It can't wait. I'm the farm manager. My father isn't here to do it. I have to deal with it. It's my responsibility in his absence.'

'It will still be there tomorrow. Or the next day. You've just come out of hospital for God's sake. You're hurt. Look at the place. Look at what's left of it. You were in there.' He planted his hands on his hips and kicked the ground with the toe of his boot, sending debris from the fire flying, anger cocktailing with fear. 'You almost died. I nearly lost you.'

'But I didn't die, and you lost me a long time ago. I have to deal with now and tomorrow and whatever the hell else follows on from this. I'm the one with the burns, Baker. I'm the one without a home, a father who's gone walkabout and a shitload to deal with. You have the luxury of running home to Baker's Hill and playing happy families with normal — a mother who bakes and is a pillar of the community, a father who supports and consults. And I have … this.' She swept a hand across the desecrated view in front of them, anger flushing her pale cheeks.

If it wasn't for the crack in her voice on that last word and the tears in her eyes, he'd think his Tikki had grown harder than bloody concrete over the eight years she'd spent alone with her father, isolated from the community. At least it hadn't killed every emotion inside her, but she'd never taken a swipe at his family before, and that spoke of something much deeper than the pain of what she'd lost.

'What's really going on in your head, Tikki? This isn't like you. It's as if I don't know you at all these days. Who are you really?'

Her shoulders sagged as she brought her arm back to her side. 'You're right you don't know me like you used to. I don't even know who I am, but I know I'm my father's daughter and that's not something I can be proud of.'

Harley felt the weight of the statement as it left her lips. 'That's not true. Look at the crop you achieve every year with out-of-the-ark equipment. You have heaps to be proud of, but that's not what I mean.' He stepped closer and put a hand over her heart. 'What I want to know is who you are in here.'

She pushed his hand away. 'No-one. I am no-one.'

'You're wrong, Tikki. You're everything to me. And I can't let you carry on this struggle alone. Tell me what I can do to help you.'

'I've done this alone for eight years. I don't need you. Give it up, Harley. Go and find someone else to pamper. I'm sure Annie Hamilton would lap up your attention.'

She turned and walked away. With a sigh, Harley followed. No way would he let her go through that door without him. No matter how hard she tried to push him away.

The smell of burnt everything hit him face-first as he pushed open the front door for her. Heat from the fire had shattered the panels of hundred-year-old stained glass on either side. They could never be replaced. Like the friendship he'd shared with Tameka, they were broken and bent, scorched by reality.

With the electricity switched off, the old homestead was poorly lit except for the sunlight that streamed in through the windows into the smoke and soot-blackened rooms. Water from the fire hoses had done most of the damage in the front rooms. Not that there was much left to damage. What the hell had happened to all their furniture?

He remembered the hallway having a table that Mai

would put flowers on and paintings that had been part of the homestead's history since before Louis had bought it. It echoed with emptiness as their booted feet made contact with the wooden floorboards, the globe-shaped yellow chandelier suspended from the ceiling rose shattered, shards scattered over the water-stained, threadbare carpet runner, blending in with the oranges and browns of the autumn-shaded pattern.

Built long and rambling, the bedrooms and bathrooms were in the left wing and the kitchen and living areas ahead through the arch at the end of the entrance hall. On the right, the formal lounge and dining room stood empty except for a couple of armchairs and a television. The large jarrah dining table that seated ten people, hand-carved by old man Fisher in the days when he'd owned the place, was missing. Gone. A huge empty space in its place. The once heavy, rich, red velvet curtains that had framed the windows were tattered and torn — none of it fire damage.

How had her dad let the place get so run down? He'd bought it fully furnished, filled with a wealth of Wongan Creek history. Golden Acres had been set to become heritage listed when the last remaining Fisher had sold it without relatives to inherit. Red tape had held up the listing and Louis Chalmers had come to town.

Harley remembered his parents reminiscing about it years after the sale went through, wishing they'd been able to afford to buy it and turn it into the Bed and

Breakfast retreat his mum had always wanted to run. If they had, the livelihood of Bakers Hill might not be under threat now.

Tameka headed through the archway to the damaged part of the house and Harley followed. She stopped where the roof was held up by steel props under the beams.

They looked to the right into what had once been the kitchen. Behind it, the mudroom and laundry were exposed to the weather, the old iron roof collapsed, the metal laundry tub and cabinet, added in the seventies, twisted, and blackened by the flames, the ancient linoleum floor covering mottled and cracked by the heat.

Harley shivered at the sight of the damage. In the harsh light of day, it was scarily apparent how lucky she'd been to escape death. He let his hands rest on her shoulders.

'Come, Tikki. Let's get your stuff and get out of here.'

He'd expected resistance after their tiff outside, but this time she let him turn her around before shaking his hands away. Again, he let her lead the way. She hadn't wanted pampering so he wouldn't, but he could be there when she finally let herself fall apart. Bugger all the bullshit about her doing it alone. It wasn't happening in this lifetime.

He waited at the door to her room. He'd only ever

been inside it once, way before they'd discovered the difference between boys and girls.

Here the damage had been minimal. Water stains on the wall that had tracked dust down from the roof space through the cornices and onto the peeling skirting boards that secured the worn rose-patterned carpet to the floor — another relic from the past.

Against the wall opposite the window, Tameka's narrow single bed was still neatly made up. The hairbrush her hair was too short to need lay on the blue painted dresser next to it, the mirror covered in sooty grime. Wedged into the corner of the peeling frame, a tattered photograph of her, Harley and Ryan curled at the edges, the Kodachrome colours leeched from it by exposure to the light streaming into the room.

Other than the photo it was empty of anything that hinted at the real Tameka and said everything about what her life had become.

She moved across to the old wood grain wardrobe and pulled down a canvas barrel bag from the top of it. Harley took the bag and held it open while she pulled shirts off hangers, jeans off neat piles on the shelf, and stuffed them into the bag.

He'd expected to see a closet full of clothes — practical ones because she wasn't a dressy kind of girl — but it seemed Tameka hadn't been shopping for an extraordinarily long time. By the time the medium-sized barrel bag was full, her wardrobe was empty.

Besides the smell of smoke and ashes, the house stood eerily and uncomfortably quiet, the only sound the flap of the yellow tarp on the roof and the creak of the rafters from the wind. The starkness of the rooms, the gloom of the blackened walls and the lingering atmosphere of despair and devastation had Harley's feet itching to leave. To get Tameka away from the depressing sight, out into the sunshine and fresh air again.

In spite of his own problems with ruined crops, the threat of foreclosure and the future of Bakers Hill in jeopardy, her challenges were proving a hell of a lot worse than his.

Tameka walked over to the dresser and tugged the photo from the frame. For a long moment, she stared at it, her fingers tracing Ryan's face. His mum had taken the photo with her new Nikon, Harley remembered.

The three of them had been playing hide and seek on Bakers Hill that day. Mum had fed them Vegemite sandwiches and snapped the shot of their grubby faces and cheesy grins. Moments before he and Tameka had wandered off down to the dam to muck around in the water.

Ryan hadn't wanted to go. He'd wanted to explore the rusty old ute in Mr C's shed. Pretend he was fixing it up.

You can't, Ry. My dad will skin you alive if he finds you in his shed.

He won't catch me. I'll be quiet.

Tikki's right, Ry. You should come with us.

Water's too cold, shrimp. You go. I'll catch up with you later.

They'd left him, but Ryan had been right, the water was freezing so they'd only stayed a while. It couldn't have been more than fifteen minutes later that Tameka had gone home and Harley had run off to find his dad to see if he could score a ride on the tractor.

The next time he'd seen his brother that day, Ryan had been covered from head to toe in a white sheet stained with sooty black fingerprints, and ash from Mr C's shed fire was still drifting down from the sky.

Chapter Twelve

'We should go, Tikki.'

Tameka looked up from studying the photo, catching the shiver Harley shrugged off and the crack in his voice. She pushed the picture into the pocket of her trackpants.

'Yeah. The insurance paperwork can wait one more day.'

Loki loped into the room, leaving sooty paw prints over the roses on the carpet, a charred wooden spoon clenched in his jaws. He dropped it at Tameka's feet.

She knelt on the floor to scratch his ears, wincing as the skin on her back pulled tight inside the suit. 'Found some treasure, boy?' Probably the spoon she'd been cooking with.

'Thinks he's a bloody Golden Retriever.' Harley

bent to pick up the spoon and studied it. He handed it back to Loki who took it and ran off. 'Not much left of that spoon.' He held out a hand and helped her to her feet. 'I couldn't have faced another white sheet, Tikki.'

Tameka's breath hitched as she stood close to him. The memory of the burning shed, her father coming out and padlocking the door. He'd walked away across the field down to the river, a leisurely stroll as if the shed behind him wasn't engulfed in flames.

And her eight-year-old-self had watched, terrified, frozen behind the big gum tree until the old iron shed buckled in on itself. Her mum had dragged her away inside, any English she'd learnt forgotten in the panic. Mum had run for the phone and held it to Tameka.

You phone. Fire.

But why hadn't she remembered all this before? What if it was her imagination making it up? Some kind of trauma after the fire. But each time they happened, the flashbacks were clearer.

She turned her face up to Harley's. Until she was sure what she'd seen was real, she couldn't tell him about the flashbacks. That she'd lived all this time knowing that her father had been aware that Ryan was in the shed that day. That he'd left a young boy to die. That he'd left her to die the same way. Terror edged into her throat. If he came back ... Would he try again?

Harley's hand cupped her face. 'You okay?'

She nodded. 'Let's go.'

Goosebumps edged their way up her arms. Her home wasn't the haven it used to be. Had it ever been safe? She hadn't imagined the kick to her head or her father walking away from a fire. Again. Tears burned her eyes, and she blinked them back as his parting words echoed in her head.

You're weak and fucking useless, Tameka. No wonder your mother deserted you.

Harley dropped his hand from her face, picked up the duffle bag and put an arm around her shoulders to lead her out into the hallway. 'I think we both need a cup of tea.'

She didn't object to his arm around her shoulders, but kept her own crossed tightly to her chest, and let him walk her across the field, through the gate and up to the house with Loki playing chasey behind them with the wooden spoon.

'Any news from the bank on your loan?' If she didn't talk, her thoughts would drive her nuts. And in all the chaos of the last few days, she'd forgotten that she was partly responsible for ruining Harley's harvest. Another cross to carry her secrets on.

'Not yet. Greg has promised he'll do his best to stall them while I put a plan together. We just have to wait. You might want to know that some of the farmers have started a petition against your father using the herbicides. If they get enough support, they'll move to apply for a court order to stop him. They're talking about lawsuits for compensation, Tikki.'

'Are you one of them?' Humiliation seeped through her.

'No. Seeking compensation would be the answer to my financial issues, but that won't stop the same damage occurring next year. I'm not happy about what they're doing, but I can understand their frustration. You know as well as they do the back-breaking hours we put into our crops and to lose so much of it to damage … that can kill a business. Especially when some of us are competing against cheaper imports.'

'I'm so sorry, Harley. I tried so hard to make him understand the harm he was doing.' Tameka stopped at the front door and waited for him to push it open. 'I'm sorry I yelled at you earlier too.'

'I shouldn't have pushed you so hard.' He squeezed her shoulder before stepping inside. 'I'm going to have to look at alternatives to carry me through to the next harvest while the bines recover. If we can't stop your father, I'll have to find another way to protect them. I don't want hectares of greenhouses. It spoils the view. But I might not have the choice. I have a niche market I can't afford to keep and can't afford to let go either.'

If Dad didn't come back it would be a blessing for everyone, the ideal solution to the problem. There'd be no more spraying, no more damage. But she'd be living in fear every time footsteps sounded on the veranda, or a car came up the drive. Golden Acres was her responsibility now. She had to fight for what she had left. Or abandon it completely. That thought scared her more than the possibility her father would walk back through the door.

'What will you do?' She followed him to the laundry where he tipped out the duffle bag and began stuffing her clothes into the washing machine. 'I can do that. Here, let me.'

He hesitated a moment as if he was about to protest, but she gave him the eye and he stepped back. It was bad enough he'd seen her charity undies, but no way would she let him handle the threadbare tradie-strength ones she wore daily. No sexy, silky lingerie, just practical working-girl cotton briefs. No-one got to see them except her anyway.

'Righto.' He leaned back against the doorframe, taking up far too much space in the narrow laundry room. 'I've kinda got a plan in my head, but it depends on how much red tape I have to cut through.'

She measured out the powder and softener from the containers in the laundry tub and tried to ignore the heat he radiated. 'Oh yeah? What?'

Harley shrugged and crossed his arms over his chest. Her hand shook a little as she looked away and poured the softener into the dispenser. Damn him for having grown into his muscles and being this solid, strong bloody tower whose walls she wanted to climb and hide behind.

'I've started on an application proposal for a rural research and development grant. After what happened to the crop, I thought if I could investigate ways on how to combat spray drift from herbicides, I could find a way to prevent it from damaging future harvests. We're struggling here, desperate to hang onto anything we can. The gold mine is expanding along with the population. The need for land to rezone to residential is growing, and John Bannister is capitalising on every aspect. Only a handful of farmers in the region want to hang on to what they have. The rest are considering selling out, taking the money, and starting over somewhere else, or giving up completely.'

Tameka drew down the lid of the top loader and set it to wash. 'That would change the whole face of the region.' Sadness warred with humiliation. Generations of farms would be lost. Rolling fields and livelihoods would disappear. And in the middle of it all, her father would have played a leading role in the downturn in the area.

'Exactly. And there's no point turning to vegetable production either. The market is seeing increased imports from the States, Italy, and China. But the real problem is that whatever we grow, spray drift will always be a problem unless we can change our methods.'

She grimaced. Surely somewhere in all of this there had to be a positive. 'And with farmers like Dad still hanging onto the old ways of control, it will remain a threat.'

Harley reached out and rubbed her arm gently. 'Not just your dad. Here's the thing … I read a report on the internet that almost sixty thousand hectares of crops in Australia are damaged by phenoxy spray drift every year.'

Tameka let out a whistle, her stomach sinking further. 'That's huge.'

Harley pushed away from the doorframe and his fingers hooked into the belt loops of his jeans. 'Estimated at around twenty million dollars before the season is even complete. A cost like that could wipe out the industry. This is the worst season on record for crop damage according to that report.'

'And the weeds are out of control which means grains farmers are spraying more.' Guilt weighed heavily in the face of the facts. Facts her father could have taken into consideration and made the necessary changes to accommodate. If he'd cared enough for the community.

Harley nodded. 'And you know what that means, right?'

'Yep. More drift, more damage.' She brushed past him and made her way to the kitchen, filling the kettle and setting it to boil. Tea. Strong and black because today the knocks just kept coming, and powerless was a feeling she was too familiar with.

'Right. So, there's this agronomist who works with farmers to get the best out of their land and looks at alternatives to current methods. So, I thought if I contact him, we could maybe work together on new organic technology that will have the same long-term effects as herbicides.'

It would be so easy to get swept up by his enthusiasm and be carried away by his plans, but she couldn't afford to lose her heart to the hope of being part of it. 'Sounds expensive.' She rinsed the mugs they'd used earlier and dropped a tea bag in each.

'Not as expensive as us losing crop growth every year. Spray drift affects broadleaf crops, so even Liv Waterman's grapevines across the creek would have suffered some damage.'

And the Chalmers' were the last of the growers in the region using phenoxies. Something she had tried to explain to her father in his less-heated, more receptive moments. All had fallen on stubbornly deaf ears.

'I try, Harley. I monitor weather conditions, check wind speeds to minimise spray drift as much as I can. But when I'm reduced to hiring a crop duster because we don't have our own, I'm limited to how much control I have over it.'

Especially when Dad insisted on aerial dusting. When he refused to consider using a less invasive way, like a boom sprayer. Almost as if he wanted to damage neighbouring crops. Maybe he did, and God knew he was angry and resentful enough to do it for reasons only he knew.

Harley stepped closer, his warmth at her back. 'I know you do, but it would be great if you stopped it altogether.'

And it wouldn't make a damn difference if she couldn't convince her father to try alternative methods. If he ever came back from wherever he'd disappeared to. Tameka stirred a little sugar into the tea.

Harley dragged a hand through his hair. 'That's why I need this research grant.' She held out a mug of tea and he took it. 'Will you help me with the proposal?'

'Harley …'

If her dad came back and found them together, who knew what he'd do. Plus, there was this memory of Ryan. If she'd seen what she thought she had, Harley would hate her for keeping quiet all these years. He'd hate her mother for not speaking up that day.

And the consequences of the truth coming out … She had to be sure of her facts, but how could she when there were only two people who knew the truth, and one was missing while the other was a potential murderer.

Harley put his mug down on the kitchen table and placed his hands on her shoulders. 'Please, Tikki?'

'Didn't I ask you to stop calling me that?' Because when he did, it made her want to close her arms around his waist and taste his mouth on hers again, to forget the years and obstacles between them.

'I'll stop calling you that if you help me put the proposal together.'

'That's blackmail.' The kind that made her lips twitch from the memory of the times when him saying her name that way could get him almost anything he wanted.

'Call it payment in lieu of accommodation for as long as you need it.'

He stepped into her space and her hands drifted up intent on pushing him away, but the moment they made contact with his shirt and the soft flannel material, she knew she'd be lost if he kissed her. And the connection between her brain and her nerve endings seemed to have short-circuited because she found herself leaning closer, tipping up her chin and wishing he would do just that.

He ran his hands down her arms, resting them on her hips and tugged her closer. His head descended and he whispered, 'Please?'

She forgot her answer as his lips moved over hers and she sank into his chest because her muscles lost the strength to hold her up. He kissed her slowly until she thought she'd melt from the controlled heat and a fire of a different kind that burned through her body. The same fire that had burnt that day in his ute, only stronger and more desperate.

When he held her closer still, she wrapped her arms

around his waist, felt the heat of his hands through the material of her trackpants and his reaction that told her Harley's body remembered hers well.

He lifted his head and rested his forehead against hers. That tender, caring thing he did — had always done — while he waited for permission to take it further. Except this time, it was him who called a halt.

'It's been a long day for you, Tikki.'

She nodded, battling between being angry with him and taking matters into her own hands. Hands that reached even now for the waistband of his jeans where she tucked her fingers inside, holding him closer for a little while longer, thinking about how easy it would be to get naked, right here and now, and lose herself in everything Harley.

Until she remembered her onesie and the damage on her back and heard the cheerful tooting of a horn coming up the unsealed driveway.

Harley swore and lifted his head. 'That'll be Mum and Dad. Their timing is impeccably awkward as usual. I've run out of bloody space in the freezer, so I hope she hasn't brought any more food.'

Tameka released her grip on his jeans and looked up at him. 'Thank you.'

'For what?'

'For being there. I've missed having you around.'

He looked at her for a long moment before releasing his hold on her arse and stepping back. 'I've missed being there for you.' He turned and walked down the hallway to the front door.

Tameka gripped the back of a kitchen chair and wondered how she could look his parents in the face with the memory of what had happened to Ryan rattling around in her head and having lost her heart to Harley all over again.

Chapter Thirteen

'Tameka love, how are you?' Shirley bustled into the kitchen loaded with shopping bags which she lined up on the kitchen table.

'I'm okay, thanks.'

Harley's mum hugged her, careful not to touch her back. 'Goodness me, you gave us a scare. You've got a little more colour in your cheeks since I saw you at the hospital. How are those burns healing up?'

Tameka shrugged off the memory of what had put the colour in her face only moments earlier. 'It's all going good.'

'And your head?' Shirley touched the bruised area around the white bandage on Tameka's temple with gentle fingers.

'Tender but better.'

'That's a nasty bruise, sweetheart.'

'It will heal.' Tameka stepped away from the warmth and love she didn't deserve. Shirley had always been so kind to her, almost like a second mum even after she'd lost her eldest son. She wouldn't feel that way when the truth came out. 'Would you like a cup of tea, Mrs B?'

'In a minute, love. I've brought you a couple of things I thought might be a better fit than the emergency supplies we gave you at the hospital.'

'Oh, you didn't have to do that. Harley and I rescued my clothes from the homestead.'

Shirley waved away her protest and dipped her hand into a bag. She pulled out a handful of neatly folded, lacy undies. 'Here we go. These are much better than those awful stripy things. I got a bargain at this lovely little shop in Perth.' She winked and held up a barely-there lacy triangle. 'Feel that love. You wouldn't even know you're wearing it.'

Tameka touched the buttery soft lace and had to admit Shirley was right. She took the scrap of lace and turned it over in her hands, enjoying the luxurious feel of the material in a colour that wasn't her usual beige.

Harley and his dad stepped into the kitchen as Shirley held out more of the same in assorted colours. Harley's eyebrows shot into his hairline at the same time heat crept into Tameka's cheeks. She scrunched the tiny triangle into her fist. But Shirley who'd been a farmer's wife for far too long to be embarrassed turned to show the men her bargain haul.

'What do you think, Harley? Much better than what Tameka has at the moment, right?'

'Very nice, Shirl. I hope you picked up a few pairs for yourself while you were there.' Mr B peeked into the shopping bags and pulled out a bra to match the undies. 'Yeah, too small for you.'

'Tom! Put that back.'

He dropped it back in the bag and grinned. Horrified and feeling her face flame with embarrassment, Tameka looked at Harley. He smiled, the bastard.

'Very nice, Mum. I'll get Tikki to model them for me later.'

'No, I bloody won't.'

Shirley patted Tameka's arm. 'Oh, he's teasing you, love. Stop it, Harley. Here, these will need to be washed. I can hear the washing machine going already so add that to the pile.' She shoved them into his hands. 'Don't forget to take the tags off first. And put them into one of those mesh laundry bag things so they don't get all messed up.'

A frustrated scream built inside Tameka. She didn't want these people's kindness or their well-meaning charity. She didn't deserve it. Irritation edged along her nerve endings, and she clenched her teeth against it. They meant well. The Bakers were nice people. It was Shirley's nature to nurture. Tameka's short nails bit into her palms. It wasn't their fault she wasn't used to kindness and nurturing.

Harley's smile turned to a frown, and he stepped closer. His fingers pried hers loose to free the undies from her fist. He added it the haul in his other hand. 'It's okay, Tikki. You don't have to take them or wear them,' he told her quietly.

She nodded because the lump in her throat wouldn't let words out of her mouth. She wouldn't cry. And she wouldn't admit that she'd like to model that underwear for Harley and have him take it off her.

Nor would she acknowledge that what she really wanted to do was throw herself into Shirley Baker's arms, cry until she had no tears left and tell her everything so she could feel the love of a mother again. Someone other than the man she loved telling her everything would be alright.

What the hell was wrong with her? She wasn't a bloody sook who cried for nothing. She hadn't cried since the day her father had torn her and Harley apart, since the beating she'd received that left her bruised and broken, since her mother had walked out the door and never looked back.

But even as she gazed into Harley's face, the tears formed in her eyes and spilled over her cheeks. Her lips quivered like a God damn baby's, and when Harley's arms went around her, undies and all, big brave independent Tameka Chalmers fell apart and sobbed into his damn shirt.

'Bloody hell, Tikki. After all you've been through,

sexy undies bring you undone?' One hand smoothed over her hair while the other clenched in a fist around the underwear and rested on the curve of her bum.

'Screw you, Baker.'

'Any other time I'd take you up on that offer, baby, but right now with your snot on my shirt, I'll pass thanks.' His lips pressed against her temple above the bruise.

She thumped a fist against his chest, not hard enough because her hand was trapped between them. Damn him for remembering that soothing, comforting words had never worked on her, that they only made her cry harder. For knowing her far too bloody well.

'You wouldn't know what to do with a girl like me.' Except he did. He knew exactly what she needed.

'If that's a challenge, we can head for the bedroom right now and I'll happily help you out of that onesie.'

'Harley Baker!' Shirley's voice came between them. 'Have you forgotten your parents are in the room?'

'How could he, dear, with you yelling at him like that?' Tom opened the fridge. 'Got any beer in here, son?'

'You are not having a beer, Tom. Alcohol is bad for your heart.'

'You didn't see the news on telly then. Scientists reckon a beer a day is good for you. I'm just helping them with their research.'

Tameka ignored their banter, grateful that they'd

turned a blind eye to her meltdown and lifted her head to look at Harley. 'Thank you.'

'You're welcome. Okay now?'

She nodded. She had to be. There was no other choice. Harley held on until she wriggled out of his hold. 'I need some air. I'll be outside.'

Loki hauled himself up out of his resting position under the table and trailed behind her down the hallway. Tameka grabbed Harley's puffer jacket off the peg and threw it around her shoulders. With the sun heading towards late afternoon, the air would be cooler down by the dam. That's where she did her best thinking with the water lapping at the shore, the birds in the trees and the soothing sight of the sun and ripples of wind on the water to ease the tension from her neck.

Clutching the edges of the jacket and wriggling into its warmth, she followed the familiar path across the Baker's field, through the gate onto Golden Acres and down to the dam.

Still no sign of Dad's ute. She didn't know whether to be happy or afraid that he hadn't come home yet. Didn't want to think about what would happen when he did. Or if he didn't.

The homestead stood gloomy and empty with its back to the creek and the yellow tarp on the roof flapping in the breeze. If Dad hadn't kept the insurance going, they had no hope of rebuilding the damaged part of the house. She should be happy about that. This could be her ticket out.

With no money to rebuild, they'd have nowhere to live. Dad might consider selling up and she'd lose everything she'd worked so hard to keep. Perhaps then she could walk away from all this. Or he could come home and pull the trigger on his gun and end it for himself. Or both of them.

Would he even come back to check if she'd survived the fire? Or would he simply abandon the property, leaving it behind to deteriorate, believing she was dead? How long could she keep it going alone not knowing?

Perhaps she should take the coward's way out. Pick up her duffle bag from Harley's laundry floor, empty whatever cash she could find in the safe on Golden Acres and leave Wongan Creek behind.

Leave with the visions of a burning shed and flames licking at the walls of the kitchen in her head. Live with the knowledge that her father was cruel enough to walk away from a burning shed with a boy trapped inside and had hated her enough to leave her to die too.

Go on with life being angry with herself because she'd never be able to make her father love her enough to stop being a miserable, cold-hearted, empty man.

Tameka slipped her arms into the jacket sleeves and zipped it up. Warmth eased the chill from her bones. Loki barked, and she looked over her shoulder to see

Harley's mum making her way down with two thermos mugs and a packet in her hands.

She sighed. She should have guessed Shirley would follow her down to make sure she was okay. At least it wasn't Harley. He'd begun chipping away at her wall and she couldn't let him break it down again like he had in the kitchen less than ten minutes ago.

'I brought your tea down. Nice and hot. These thermal mugs are a great invention, aren't they?'

'Thank you, Mrs B.' Tameka took the mug and wrapped her frozen fingers around it. Not much heat thanks to the insulation, but what little came through gave her comfort.

'Call me Shirley, love. You're all grown up now.' She pulled a blister strip from her coat pocket. 'I brought your painkillers. Harley says you're about due for them again.'

'Thank you. I'll take them when my tea cools down.' She took the strip, quietly thankful for the painkillers. As much as she'd like to ignore the raw burn of pain that ate all the way up her back, now wasn't the time to be brave.

'Good idea. Here, have a biscuit too. Can't have you taking those things on an empty tummy.' Shirley handed her the plastic wrapper containing two tea biscuits, blew out a breath and shadowed her eyes with her hand. 'It's still so beautiful and peaceful down here by the water.'

'I'm sorry my dad took the use of the dam away from you.'

'Oh love, don't worry about that. It was his dam on his property. We were lucky to have it for as long as we did, an agreement between us and the Fishers your dad had the good grace to continue for a while.' She shrugged. 'It made us consider other options which we would have had to think about anyway if drought took hold. It was a challenge, yes, but we worked around it. We'd planned to build our own dam, but then Tom had his heart attack and that changed things for us. But now Harley's made a start on one anyway. All we'll need when it's done is the rain to fill it.'

'But it put unnecessary stress on your business, on Mr B.' Tameka sipped her tea through the hole in the lid on the mug.

'Sweetheart, your dad closing off our pump on the dam had nothing to do with Tom's heart attack if that's what you're worried about. He was smoking a pack a day back then.' Shirley sighed. 'Bakers Hill hasn't been without its own challenges. We've had fires, too much rain, too little rain, losing Ryan ... somehow we'll survive this disaster too.'

Losing Ryan. That was the turning point in all this. The axis on which their world had spun and created the fallout to come in later years. Tameka twisted the mug in her hand.

'Can I ask you something about Ryan?'

Shirley hesitated a moment, her eyes on the flock of cockatoos pecking between the roots of the weeping willow further up the bank.

'Of course.'

'How did the fire start?' As kids, they'd never been told, and what happened that day had never been discussed in front of the children again.

'The firies found what was left of a box of matches next to Ryan when they … when they found him after the fire was out. We think he must have taken them from the house earlier that day and we don't know why. It didn't make sense at the time because Ryan never liked fire. He hated that Tom smoked. He didn't even like those sparkler things or candles on his birthday cake.' She sipped her tea quietly for a moment. 'Who knows why he had the matches with him in the shed. Maybe he took them to stop Tom from lighting the next cigarette.'

The hitch in Shirley's voice made her own throat ache. Tameka hated to raise what must still be painful memories for a mother who'd lost her son in such tragic circumstances, but the need to find out if her memory was real or not ate at her mind. And if it was real, she'd have to cope with the fact that her father was guilty of murdering an innocent boy. She already knew he was mean enough to. Had he deliberately abandoned her to the fire or had he thought she would simply get up off the floor and save herself?

'How come Ryan couldn't get out of the shed when the fire started?'

Shirley twirled the mug to cool the tea. Or perhaps she was buying time before answering. 'Your dad said he'd been to the shed earlier to get some fertiliser. He knew you kids were playing around in the fields, so he put the padlock on the door after he dragged it shut. He didn't want you getting in there with all the poisons and fuel stored in the shed.'

That didn't make sense at all. When she'd seen her father lock the door, the shed was already on fire. But how reliable was that memory?

'He didn't see or hear Ryan inside the shed?'

That would make sense though because Ryan would have stayed quiet knowing her dad would be super angry finding him in there when he'd forbidden them to play in the shed.

'No. The firies think Ryan might have lit a match to find his way out in the dark, fallen over and dropped it. With so much fuel in the shed, the fire took hold quickly.' Shirley raised a hand and dabbed at her eyes with her fingers, her words catching in her throat.

Tameka's throat ached with tears she couldn't cry. A part of her didn't want to ask any more questions, didn't want to hurt Shirley any further, but until she could lay Ryan's ghost to rest in her head, the memory of what she thought she'd seen would continue to haunt her. 'Why did the firies think Ryan fell over and dropped the match?'

'When they did a post-mortem examination, they found he had a crack in his skull. The coroner ruled that he'd fallen, hit his head, and was knocked unconscious which is why he couldn't call for help and no-one knew he was there … until after.'

Exactly as she had been when the fire in the kitchen had raged behind her father's departing back. A sick feeling settled in her stomach, Tameka knew she wouldn't be able to shake it until she found out the truth.

'I'm so sorry, Shirley.'

'It was an accident, sweetheart. A terrible, tragic accident. Tom still blames himself for not hiding the matches out of reach. I blame myself for not keeping a closer eye on the boys that day.' She sighed, the sound released on a shaky breath. 'What made you think of it after all this time? You and Harley were so little, barely eight years old. Was it the fire?'

Tameka shrugged against the unease that crept up her spine. Clearly there would be someone else to blame if what she remembered was true. 'I guess the fire brought it all back. If it wasn't for Harley and Loki coming to my rescue …'

She'd be dead too. Just like Ryan. And it wouldn't have been a tragic accident. It would have been murder.

Chapter Fourteen

arley tried to concentrate on what his dad was saying and not worry about Tameka. The fire, her dad's absence following it, the stark emptiness of the homestead and her reluctance to talk about anything — the combination clawed at his gut. Instinct told him something was off, and it had nothing to do with the years of cold war between the Chalmers and the Bakers.

He didn't want to believe that her dad had abandoned her, but his prolonged disappearance was odd, even for a man who'd isolated himself from the community. Had never really been part of it. He'd seldom left the farm ever and certainly not for more than a couple of hours at a time when he did.

Then there was the uneasiness of what would happen when he came back. If he came back at all. Her dad had always been unpredictable and how he would respond to finding his daughter staying at Bakers Hill was cause for concern and no doubt fodder for the gossip mill.

But she was probably safer with him than anywhere else because he wouldn't hesitate to put old man Chalmers on his arse if he did anything to hurt Tameka. Harley wasn't a green nineteen-year-old anymore, and he would do whatever it took to protect her if she needed it.

His dad's hand descended on his shoulder, a reminder that he was there. 'You're not listening to me, are you, son?'

Harley uncrossed his arms and hooked his thumbs into the belt loops on his jeans. 'Sorry, Dad. It's been a hell of a week.'

'Sure has. The unrest about the extent of the crop damage this year is growing and tempers along with it. Add to that John Bannister pestering everyone into selling and Wongan Creek has seen more pub brawls in the last week than it has in years between those fighting to stay and those wanting to go. I hope it settles down soon. Louis Chalmers' actions have turned the whole town in on themselves.'

'Not a good thing to see, is it? Not when we all need to be putting our heads together to find a solution.' If he could turn the clock back a week, he would. But there'd still be no guarantee that none of this would have happened.

Dad took a sip of his beer. 'We'll need to consider our options moving forward. The area has been in decline for a while now. It's not just the growth of the mine or the spray drift killing our industry. The expense of farming has become too great. Dairy farmers are losing out to cheaper supermarket milk from the east. Too many new diseases are finding their way into crops, the expense of harvest and transport to market, the effects of climate change — no way can we compete with cheaper imports when their cost of production is less than half of what ours is.'

'Yeah, I know. I spoke to someone at the Department of Agriculture during the week. Times are changing for farmers. Farming in general really. How long can we continue to hold down second jobs while trying to keep our farms afloat? Times are tough. Consumers are counting their pennies.' And he needed to hold onto his monopoly on the hops market or lose everything.

'We've got to change with the times, son. We need to turn our crop to something more viable.'

'If Greg can keep the wolves from the door long enough, I had it in my mind to open up our own brewery on the farm. Cultivate my own yeast. We could open the house up to the Bed and Breakfast idea Mum always wanted. It's just me and Loki in the house with five bedrooms and two extra bathrooms standing empty.'

The more he thought about it, the more excited he got. It had been ages since he could sink his teeth into a new project. And maybe, just maybe, Tameka would be around to share it with him. Because damn it, when old man Chalmers did show up, Harley would do everything he could to keep her safely away from the old bastard.

Tom nodded. 'Your mum would like that. I reckon she'd be happy to come on board with the breakfast part. With the need for short term accommodation growing for the mineworkers, which would provide a small solution to the immediate housing issues. Definitely worth thinking about, son. What else have you considered?'

'I've been reading up on the cause and effect of spray drift. I'm working on a proposal to apply for a research grant looking at organic alternatives to the use of herbicides and pesticides. That would at least take care of a portion of the field where I can carry out testing.'

'Still won't bring in an income though, would it?'

'Not initially, no. I'd still need a backup crop or alternative plan. We need the income now. God knows how long the grant would take to come through. Even going with the Bed and Breakfast idea and adding the brewery, we could be wading through red tape for months trying to get licences. We were doing okay until this harvest turned to shit.' He didn't have the heart to tell his dad the cost of the crop he couldn't harvest that now lay rotting in the compost bins.

Tom tapped his chin the way he did when the wheels turned thoughts and possibilities over in his mind. 'But that's not all that's on your mind, is it?'

Harley shook his head. 'Tameka's dad hasn't been seen since the night of the fire. Don't you find that odd, Dad? I do. What man leaves his farm during planting season for no reason when there is so much work to do?'

'Hmmm, now there's a difficult bastard.'

'Dad, I keep thinking that maybe the fire wasn't an accident.'

'That's grasping at straws, Harley. Tameka was quite clear in her statement to Barry Metcalfe that it was an accident and that her father wasn't in the house at the time.'

Harley turned the beer bottle in his hands. It had gone warm with the bottle still three-quarters full. 'But she doesn't know where he's gone or when he'll be back.'

'Yeah, that's a bit odd. Even back when you kids were little, he hardly ever left the farm. If they needed something in town, Mai would take Tameka and go in, even if it was parts for the machines or the pumps.'

'What was he like, Dad? I remember him always

being bad-tempered and impatient. Was he ever abusive or violent?'

'He was never a friendly bloke, but we never saw or heard of anything that led us to believe he was anything more than just a difficult man.' Tom scratched his head. 'No-one was surprised when Mai walked out on him. We had a fairly good working relationship, I guess. He got on with his farm and I got on with mine. Our only real confrontation was the nonsense over the dam, a typical knee-jerk reaction from Chalmers. And there was a bit of nastiness over the shed fire … and Ryan.'

Harley sighed, patting his father's shoulder as his breath hitched on Ryan's name. Losing him still hurt so much even after almost twenty years. 'Yeah, if only we could go back in time, Dad. I can't help but think Tameka's not telling the whole truth.'

'About the fire?'

'About a lot of things.'

'Hard to say when you haven't really been close since you were nineteen. Many things changed that day, son.'

And Harley regretted every moment since. 'If I could change what happened …'

'Hindsight. It's a bitch. Look, your mum and I always expected you and Tameka to get together. It was inevitable. After Ryan died, you two were even closer and we were glad about that because it got you through.'

Funny how he couldn't remember Tameka's dad

having a problem with that, but they were kids and oblivious to what the adults were doing when there were lizards to catch and trees to explore. They'd simply stayed out of the way until they were needed to help. 'So why the extreme reaction from her dad when we did get together then? I've never quite understood it.'

His dad shrugged. 'Who knows why Chalmers did anything. He grew grumpier and more difficult to deal with every year. After the incident with the dam, we gave up any pretence of friendship and let him get on with it.'

'Why do you think Mai didn't take Tameka with her when she left?'

'That's the question on everyone's lips and the answer would be pure speculation. Maybe Tameka chose to stay? She was nineteen, legally an adult. But that doesn't make sense either when she and Mai were so close.'

'And Mai's never been seen again.' A chill crept up Harley's spine.

'Now you're letting your imagination run away with you, son. Mai didn't speak English very well. She didn't quite fit into the community despite everyone's best efforts. Even Ahn at the hardware store couldn't bring her out of her shell, and she spoke Mai's language. She wasn't a happy lady. Chalmers wasn't impressed because she hadn't given him a son. Everyone knew it wasn't a love-match. He might even have put her on a plane back to Vietnam himself. It's not something we'll ever know the answer to.'

Dad was more than likely right, but Harley couldn't stop the questions from forming in his head. What kind of mother walked away from her child, grown up or not? His mum wouldn't. But the only one who could answer that question was Tikki and he wasn't about to ask.

Harley watched as his mum and Tameka made their way through the gate and back up onto Bakers Hill with Loki darting all over the place. Maybe he should consider getting another dog, a companion to help calm Loki down or he'd never make a good farmhand.

Mum had her arm through Tameka's, and their heads were close together like they were sharing a secret the way only women could. Dad stepped up beside him.

'Neither of them would have had an easy life with Chalmers, Harley. It may be better if her old man has taken off.'

'What would happen to the farm then?'

Dad shrugged. 'If it owes money to the bank, it will be repossessed, I guess. Or it will just stay in limbo until he's confirmed dead.'

Which meant Tameka would be living in limbo indefinitely too unless her father showed up. 'I don't know what to do, Dad.'

'Not much you can do except be there for as long as

she'll accept your help.' He cupped his hands around his mouth. 'Hey, Shirl! Shake it up. We need to go.'

His mum waved and they walked a little faster.

'I don't like driving after dark since the heart attack. Has Tameka filed a missing person's report with Sergeant Riggs?'

'I've offered to report it, but she doesn't want to make a fuss.' Harley rocked on his feet. 'I think she's hoping he'll show up in his own time. Or maybe not at all.'

'Fair enough. The girl's got enough on her plate as it is. Maybe she knows where he is, but they just need a break from each other, hey?' Tom patted Harley's shoulder.

'Don't you think it's odd that he disappears on the night his daughter almost dies in a fire?'

'When has Chalmers done anything that wasn't odd? He bought Golden Acres, walked into this town with no past and a pregnant foreign bride on his arm, and started farming. No-one knows where he came from, and he kept it that way.'

'Even in a town this small where everyone knows your business? No-one asked?'

His dad shrugged. 'They didn't need to. He didn't cause trouble with the locals except for not supporting them in business, and still flies under the gossip radar. People are curious, but there's always been enough going on in town to keep their focus off him. Whether he's here or not won't make any difference because from what I hear that girl keeps the farm running.'

'There are so many things I don't understand, Dad.'

'The answers will find a way to the surface, son. They always do. You just need to be patient with the girl. Since she's come to you for help instead of shacking up at the caravan park, I'd say she'll tell you when she's good and ready.'

Harley watched as his mum and Tameka took the stairs up onto the veranda. Her cheeks were pale, and her lips pulled tight. She looked tired. He wanted to sweep her up and lie her down then curl around her and keep her safe, make all the horrors of the last few weeks — hell, years — disappear.

She stood close without touching him as they waved his parents away and then they were alone with questions rolling around in his mind and Tameka seemingly lost in her own thoughts as silence stretched between them.

'Everything okay?' He let his gaze trace her pale, drawn face.

She nodded. 'I'm a little tired. I think I might lie down for a while.'

'Sure. Call me if you need anything, okay? And take Loki with you. He looks like he could do with a nap.' Loki leaned against her as if he'd fall over when she moved. Harley had an awful feeling he wasn't the only one who'd lost his heart to the girl next door.

Chapter Fifteen

Tameka shuffled through the papers on the desk in the manager's office on Golden Acres. She'd had a rough night, tossing and turning, torn between discomfort and the worry of what state the farm was really in. So, she'd snuck out early right after breakfast to get a head start on hunting down paperwork.

Thankfully, the office had escaped most of the fire damage and besides everything being covered in fine black soot, she'd been able to salvage most of the accounts scattered across the desktop. And wished she hadn't.

A couple of hours work sorting through invoices left her with a pile of paper covered in red or green 'overdue' stickers. Thousands of dollars outstanding for fertilisers and general supplies and judging by the amount owing on the electricity bill, they were lucky they still had power. No wonder Dad hadn't let her near the accounts. She held little hope that he'd paid the insurance bill.

Yep, there it was. Unpaid with a note that cancellation was imminent. Three months ago. Is that why Dad had walked away from the burning house?

'Damn it, Dad.'

Tameka tossed the pile of paperwork back onto the desk. She should have paid more attention to what he was doing, sneaked in a look while he was passed out in his armchair. But she'd been too exhausted to think after a day out in the field or the long trips away for supplies that could have been sourced in Wongan Creek.

Dad had stood firm on his resolution not to support the locals and now she knew the reason why. He'd been stringing creditors along all the way from Kalgoorlie to Perth. How many more nasty surprises were hiding between the walls of the office? Golden Acres was bank-snatch away from going belly-up.

In the distance, an engine rumbled and fear congealed like cold porridge in her stomach. If this was Dad coming back, she was alone and unprotected. God knew what state of mind he'd be in, and she'd never been this afraid of him before — a cold, raw fear that if he found her alone he'd finish what he'd started. Loki had deserted her to find Harley, so any chance he'd behave like a guard dog was lost.

She reached for the top drawer on the desk and pulled it out, her fingers searching underneath for the spare key to the gun safe. Moving quickly, she opened the safe and grabbed the spare rifle and buckshot. Her fingers fumbled over loading it.

Even if it wasn't Dad, it could be looters who thought the burnt-out homestead would be fair game. Not that there was much left of the contents to loot. If it was Dad, the crazy she'd seen in eyes on the night of the fire called for caution.

Tameka shivered. Not that she was sure she could ever shoot him, but hopefully, the threat alone would be enough. A big man, strong and out of control in a temper, he'd already proven he had the strength to overpower her.

Harley's ute came into view, and she breathed a sigh of relief. Stepping out on the veranda, she kept the rifle in her hand pointed to the ground, the safety on.

No threat physically, but emotionally Harley had power over her she didn't want right now. Not when her heart was so close to being his again. Not until she'd sorted through the mess in her head. Maybe never.

He pulled to a stop, swinging the nose of the ute to face back up the road he'd come in on. He got out, Loki bouncing out behind him before he slammed the door closed. His hands went to his hips, hitching up the red and black-checked flannel shirt tails as he leaned back against the tailgate, one booted foot up on the bumper, the other planted firmly in the red dust. He scratched Loki's ears before letting the dog run up to Tameka.

'I come in peace. With beer.' Harley held up his hand making a V with his fingers. 'Don't shoot.'

Tameka felt a smile tug at her lips, the tension in her neck and shoulders easing a little. 'Anyone who can pull off a Vulcan salute with such ease is safe by my standards.'

'And I thought the beer was the deal-breaker.'

'Probably not a great idea to wash down painkillers and antibiotics with beer.'

'Good point.' He turned around and hauled a small blue icebox and a shopping bag out of the back of the ute. 'That's why the beer's for me and the tea is for you. And I brought some of the Danishes Mum hauled in last night. I figured you'd need sustenance about now with all this dust and soot around.'

'You know your way into a girl's heart, Harley.' And damn it, he did. Even after all this time apart, he was tuned in to her. He'd know she was afraid, uneasy, unsettled. He'd taken care of it with tea and a Danish and bringing her back his dog for company. In another time, another world … but dreams were cheap when reality cost more than you could give.

He smiled that heart-stopping smile that lifted the corners of lips she wanted on hers every morning and every night and a good portion of the day in between. 'Permission to board?'

'Permission granted.' But she'd keep the line drawn in the sand, even if he did come armed with tea. 'I hope that brew's hot.'

He dropped the esky and the bag on the top step of the veranda. His gaze pinned hers. 'Hot and strong with a hint of milk and a touch of Jasmine.'

Tameka looked away, crossed her arms, and toed the wooden deck of the veranda with her boot. 'You're a dag, Harley Baker, but your lines don't work on me.' But damn him, they did because what girl in her right mind wouldn't melt in a puddle at his feet when he turned up the wattage on that smile?

'A dag who brings Danish and tea.' He rubbed a thumb across her cheek. 'You have a streak of dirt on your face.'

Her heart did a little happy dance at the brush of his skin on hers. She should slap his hand away. Except his palm cupped her face, his head tilted to the side then his lips brushed where his thumb had been and her eyes fluttered closed as he trailed a kiss across her cheek.

'Gone now,' he whispered against her ear.

Her fingers tightened around the rifle to stop them reaching for him and dragging him closer, taking that kiss a step further.

'You're in my space.' Tameka tried to keep the purr out of the reprimand and failed.

He drew back a little, tipped up her chin with his fingers and grinned. 'I kissed a girl ... and I liked it.'

She rolled her eyes. 'Really? Katy Perry? Seriously? Scrap the dag. You're a douchebag.' Tameka gave him a little shove even though her heart pounded away because she liked him kissing her too. 'Can I have that tea before it gets cold?'

'Princess Tameka, you can have anything you damn well want.' Harley lifted the flask of tea from the shopping bag and held it out to her before sitting down on the top step. He patted the empty space beside him. 'Come and sit on your throne beside me.'

How many years had it been since they'd played this game of make-believe? Where they were king and queen of the land, and they'd sat on the top step of the house at Bakers Hill looking over what was theirs. Happier times. Ryan had never wanted to be a part of their game. He'd take his sandwich and go potter around in the machinery shed instead. Ryan …

Tameka sat next to Harley on the step and opened up the flask to pour tea into the plastic cup. Should she tell him what she'd remembered? A wind gust stirred up around them and Tameka shivered against its icy fingers. Burnt paper and charred debris swirled along the ground before coming to rest where they fell as the wind died down again. What difference would it make? Ryan would still be dead, and she didn't know for sure that what she remembered was the truth.

Harley held out a Danish. 'Apple and custard.'

She studied the Harley-sized bite out of the top. 'You taste-tested it?'

'Someone had to and Loki's too busy killing his rope. Just looking after your health. It wouldn't do you any good if it was stale or sour, would it?' His thigh bumped against hers as he reached for his beer. 'I prefer jam, anyway.'

Tameka felt the gloom lift a little. They'd always shared their Danish, even throughout the period where boy germs sucked. Sharing that habit again came so naturally again as they sat together on the step, shoulders touching, their bodies warming each other against the chilly winter wind.

Harley sipped his beer, and she watched his throat work to take the liquid. Everything about him was beautiful and out of bounds for her, no matter how much she wanted to run her fingers down that throat and into the V of his shirt.

His gaze slid to hers and caught her looking. In true Harley style, he said nothing. Only grinned that knowing smile as he looked away and took another sip. Tameka placed her mouth on the Danish where his had been earlier and nibbled away at the pastry. They sat in silence watching the debris swirl around in the wind and finished their impromptu picnic.

Tameka drained the tea from her mug, shook it out and screwed it back in place on the flask. 'Thanks.'

'You're welcome. Hey, there's an inaugural community picnic this Sunday over the creek at The Cranky Lizard. Would you like to go? I hear Liv's daughter, Fen, has moved back here from the city. She's a great girl. You two would get along well together.'

And face the questions on everyone's lips? Hell no. There'd be more questions than ever after the fire, and her father's mysterious disappearance would only add fuel to the gossip. Not even the lure of Liv Waterman's peaceful vines and koi pond could take the edge off her reluctance to face the people of Wongan Creek so soon after the damage.

'I don't think so, Harley. I'm not sure attending a public picnic is a good idea.'

'Why not? I think it will be fun. Gold coin donation, sausage sizzle, music, dancing, and we'd be helping the community.'

How could she tell him she didn't even have a gold coin to donate? 'I can't leave the farm. There's cleaning up to do and fields to tend. I've just finished planting.'

Harley packed the remains of their snack into the shopping bag and closed up the esky. 'What? You're going to sit on the veranda and watch the seeds sprout? Pretty boring when you could be dancing among the vines with me.'

She stood and walked down the steps. 'You know I can't dance.'

'Oh, I beg to differ on that one. I remember you having some pretty awesome moves.' His lips curved in a downright cheeky grin.

Tameka gave him a little shove. 'Stop it. I'm not going. The crowds … not my thing.'

'You don't have to be afraid of them, Tikki. I've got your back.'

'They'll expect answers to questions I'm not ready to answer.'

And as much as she appreciated their kindness and how they'd seen to her needs following the fire, she simply couldn't give them anything of herself in return. Not when she'd have to take it back again when her father rolled home.

Going to the picnic would mean re-engaging with the community, chasing a dream that had never been hers to catch — being part of a warm, loving family.

And if they found out the truth about what happened to Ryan, she'd be cast out again. As quickly as they'd open their arms to her, they'd close them if her father was to blame for Ryan's death, especially if it was intentional.

'You go. I'll keep an eye on Loki for you. Do any chores that need doing while you're gone. Give all the dishes in your cupboards a good wash in case Loki missed a few.'

It was the least she could do since he'd refused to

take anything from her in return for the roof over her head. And now that she'd seen the state of their accounts, she could never pay him anyway.

'I don't want you overdoing it. You need to rest and let those burns heal. One day, Tikki, take one day out to enjoy yourself. Don't you think you deserve it?'

She toed the red dirt under her boot, her hands on the tailgate of Harley's ute. What if this was the last time she and Harley had together? The future of Bakers Hill lay in the balance. Golden Acres was all but gone. What did she have left?

If she was forced to leave Wongan Creek for good at least she could spend one last day with Harley having fun. Like old times. Surely she could deal with curiosity and gossip for one final day. Sacrifice the little that was left of her peace of mind for one day of happiness with the man who held her heart. Before she let him go again.

Harley's hand rested on her shoulder for a moment before he leaned on the ute beside her, his hip against the metal, his elbow on the rim. Close enough to feel the warmth radiate from his body and make her want to snuggle into that red and black flannel comfort.

'I'll be there with you all the time, Tikki. I won't leave your side. I'll field all the questions for you. Just come out with me. For old time's sake.'

She sighed. It would give her some time away from the farm to sort out the pictures in her head, work through the emotions of the last few days — no, years — and process all the reasons why she shouldn't let Harley back into her life now she wasn't a child any longer and her father had deserted her.

'I'll think about it.'

Chapter Sixteen

ameka's thinking was driving him nuts. For the second night in a row, Harley listened to the creak of the floorboards as she paced her room. He checked his watch. Ten o'clock. Maybe she needed a hot chocolate to help her sleep. Or chamomile tea.

God damn it, he needed chamomile tea. He raked a hand through his hair. He'd tried to remain aloof and disinterested as he'd smoothed ointment on her burns and redressed the worst ones, all the time checking on her pain levels. But Jesus, he was only human after all and thanks to the limited water supply, there were only so many cold showers he could take.

And as for getting her in and out of that bloody onesie twice a day … that really tested the limits of his libido. Sex should be the last thing on his mind with her so hurt, but damn it, all he wanted to do was hold her and celebrate that she was alive.

His mind shouted no but his body had other ideas, and she wasn't his to have. Not unless she made the first move. Then she could have him. Any which way she liked. For however long she wanted him. But for now, he had to stop her bloody thinking, or she'd drive both him and Loki crazy with her pacing.

Harley strode into the kitchen and filled the kettle with water then flicked on the switch to boil it. Hot chocolate with a chamomile tea base — for both of them. That way maybe they'd both get some sleep. And if dogs could have chocolate, he would have made one for Loki too because the damn dog paced the hallway between her door and his all night long. But of course, chocolate was poisonous to dogs so Loki would have to settle for his chamomile tea.

He spooned tea leaves into the infuser and hot chocolate into the mugs. Outside the wind howled its distaste for winter as morning crept closer. Tomorrow Tameka would have to go into Wongan Creek for her check-up. Maybe that's why she had ants in her pants tonight even though her burns were healing nicely.

Harley sighed. The National Farmers Federation had arranged a formal meeting tomorrow too. They'd called in some legal advice to deal with the fallout from the spray drift. That wouldn't be pleasant for Tameka if she ran into any unhappy attendees in town.

Soon he would have to make a decision on the future of Bakers Hill. Put that degree of his to good use and cement a plan to save it. Or lock up and leave like he'd heard of others doing in the area.

He felt rather than heard Tameka enter the kitchen. 'Hey, Tikki. Can't sleep? Do you need something for pain?'

'Nope. The wind, I guess. Why are you still up? It's almost midnight.'

Harley poured hot water into the infuser. 'Can't sleep either. I'm making hot chocolate. I was going to bring one in to you.'

'Well, I'm here now. What's on telly?'

'Reruns of old cop shows. Want your drink in there? It's a bit warmer with the fire on. I've got a blanket if you'd prefer I turn the heat off.' She'd probably be wary of flames now and snuggling under a blanket together had its own appeal.

'A blanket will be fine. I'll finish the drinks while you go dampen down the fire.'

He turned and handed her the spoon. Lack of sleep had put bruised rings under her eyes. He wished it was as simple as kissing them away. 'Deal. Chamomile tea to mix the chocolate powder.' He tapped a finger on the diffuser then pushed Loki's soup mug towards her. 'Loki has about a quarter mug of tea.'

'Seriously? He has his own mug. Your dog lives like a king.'

He looked at her for a long moment, his arms itching to hold her. He'd treat her even better than he treated his dog, who was by far his best mate at the moment. 'Imagine how I'd treat my girl.' If she'd let him.

'Don't go getting ideas, Harley.' The spoon slipped from her fingers into the mug. 'I'm sharing your blanket. That's all.'

'I know.' He'd take whatever she'd give just to have her close.

'Good.' She poured the tea into the mugs. 'Go. This is almost ready.'

Harley made his way into the lounge and dampened down the fire, closing the flue to shut off the oxygen that fed it. As the flames dwindled, the coals still glowed. There'd be enough residual heat to keep them warm until morning but there were no more flames to remind Tameka of the horror she'd survived.

Nothing to remind him of Ryan suffering the same fate, only worse. Every time he rubbed ointment on her burns, he thought of all the things he could have done to save his brother that day. Like not letting him go to the shed alone in the first place. Insisted he stay with them. But he had let his brother go. And Ryan would be gone nineteen years on Sunday.

Loki curled up on his end of the sofa with his head on the armrest. 'You're hogging the sofa again, Loki.' Harley shifted the dog's butt a little further away to make room for Tameka.

'Dibs on the middle.' Tameka carried two mugs in one hand and Loki's soup mug in the other. 'It's hot, Loki, you have to wait.'

Harley snorted. 'Fine by me. You can have the dog farting next to you the whole night. I'm all for clean air.'

'Rather dog fart than something hard in my back all night.' She caught the look on his face and interpreted it exactly as he knew she would. 'Down, boy.'

'Spoilsport.' He grinned.

'Whatever.'

She did the whole eye-roll thing he was getting familiar with seeing from her, but he spotted the tilt of her lips in a barely-there smile and resisted the urge to punch the air. *Oh yeah! Score one for Harley Baker.*

Tameka sat with her body turned a little to the side and her back away from the sofa, a reminder of her injuries that dampened the fire that burned inside Harley. He slipped in between her and the armrest, letting his shoulder take some of her weight as they watched the show on telly and sipped their hot drinks.

When her head drooped to his shoulder, he took the empty mug from her hands and put it on the floor next to the sofa. He slid lower in the seat and pulled up the blanket over them as she settled comfortably against his chest. Slipping an arm around her shoulders, he held her to him, knowing he'd get even less sleep on the sofa than he would in his bed, but it would be *so* worth it.

Tameka awoke to something a lot firmer than a mattress pressed against her from head to toe. And the hard evidence that Harley's body was very much awake even if his mind hadn't caught up yet.

Somehow she'd ended up breast-to-chest, Harley under her, her head on his shoulder and her body pressed to his, their breathing in even harmony. Loki had relocated to the floor, and they were stretched out lengthwise on the sofa. Probably a good thing otherwise they'd both have stiff necks.

She'd slept, despite the biting sting that crawled over her skin from the burns. For the first time in God knew how long. Most nights she felt as if she never closed her eyes, sleeping in spurts where the waking hours were the longest. The last time she'd slept so well was the night she'd crept out of her room window to share a sleeping bag in the back of the ute under the stars with Harley.

Tameka smiled and cuddled into his warmth. They'd been such innocents then. Their thoughts at sixteen hadn't gone past identifying the constellations in the clear skies, their trial kisses awkward fumbling of discovery. And hooley dooley, when they learnt how much they liked kissing and touching … they'd created constellations of their own and filled the skies with fireworks.

Then came the Big Bang. She curled her fist into Harley's shirt, felt his breath on her hair. Harley all around her, touching the deepest part of her, making her feel loved and wanted, alive. Making her feel like she belonged. To him. Making her wish for things, find hope for a happier future.

And in an instant those dreams were shattered. She couldn't hope to have that again. Her father had intervened then just as he would now. Eventually. When he decided to come home. And even if he didn't, the ghosts of the past were enough to keep her and Harley apart.

But she had now and Harley under her, his warmth around her and his heartbeat under her cheek. She slipped her hand under his shirt, her fingers brushing against his skin, palm over his heart.

He stirred under her touch. She pressed her lips to his throat, buried her face against the strong column of his neck and inhaled everything Harley to store in her senses for a time when she could no longer touch him.

His hand come up to touch her face as she trailed kisses along his jawline, stretching against him to reach his lips, satisfied that he wanted this as he hovered between sleep and awake. She touched her mouth to his, felt his lips move under hers, and kissed him with everything in her heart.

His fingers slipped into her hair, cupped her head, and held her there as he returned her kisses with his own. Searching, scorching kisses that set fire to every inch of skin between them. Where their hips aligned the burn was hotter, hungrier, needier.

She raised her head to find his eyes open, sleepy, and full of the only question between them. Yes or no.

'A guy could get used to waking up like this.' His voice was husky with sleep and desire. 'I'll have to make hot chocolate and share a blanket with you more often.'

Tameka pressed her fingers to his lips. Talk might change her mind. Talk was something they could do over the fence when reality came crashing through the door. 'Love me, Harley.'

His eyes searched hers, the hand on her butt pressed her closer to him. 'Are you sure?'

'Of this? Yes. Of tomorrow? No.'

'Then let's make today count.'

He kissed her until her mind spun like an out-of-control starship circling the sun and heading for the epicentre. He touched every inch of bare skin he could find, and when every nerve ending begged to be satisfied, he whispered, 'Let me help you out of that onesie.'

She smiled against his lips, opened her heart, and let him find his way inside.

Chapter Seventeen

They took the bike into town. Not the dirt bike but Harley's Heritage Softail Classic with the twin cam engine and deep throaty roar. He figured it would be less friction on her back and cause her less pain than driving in the ute. And honestly, it meant she'd be wrapped around him like she'd been this morning and now that she had been, he didn't plan on letting go. With her denim-clad legs lining his thighs and her body against his back, he could bloody ride forever.

Even with layers of denim, leather, and wool between them to keep out the chill of the wind, he felt every movement of her body against him. And blessed the cold that could freeze a duck's nuts because it would be damn embarrassing showing up at the community meeting with happy pants.

He didn't want to put Tameka through the gossip mill more than she'd already been. Showing up together probably wasn't the brightest idea to stamp out any misplaced rumours that they were back together, but they had to do what was practical. Besides, with the town preoccupied with meetings and John Bannister's methods of persuasion to sell their farms, perhaps they wouldn't even notice.

Harley backed the bike into a parking spot outside Wongan Creek's hospital. He felt the touch of Tameka's hand on his shoulder as she climbed off before removing her helmet.

'Want me to come in with you?'

She hesitated a moment. 'Um, no. It's okay. I'll meet you at the Town Hall when I'm done.'

'I can come back for you.' He didn't want her walking into the lion's den alone. Not when he didn't know where they were heading with the argument over the spray drift. With still no sign of Louis Chalmers returning, the crowd might take it into their hot heads to hold Tameka responsible.

'I can walk just fine.'

Panic squeezed his heart a little tighter. Surely she wasn't freezing him out already? He pulled off his helmet and dragged a hand through his hair. 'Okay.'

She raised a hand to touch his face, her fingers icy cold. 'I have something I need to do. Alone.'

'You don't have to be alone, Tikki.' He caught that beautiful, sad, chocolate gaze.

'I know.'

'As long as you do.' He stared at her a moment longer, studying the determined set of her chin and firmly clamped lips. He'd coax them open later. 'What are you going to do?'

She fiddled with the strap of the helmet. 'Report my father missing.'

His stomach sank. That opened a whole new crate of yabbies. Not that he wished old man Chalmers ill, but it had been damn peaceful around the place without him. And if he did come back to Golden Acres, Harley would likely lose Tameka again.

'Right.' He wanted to be there for her for that too, but the set of her shoulders and the ramrod stiffness in her spine said it all. Tameka would deal with it, and he'd be there to catch her when she fell to pieces later. 'I'll wait for you at the community meeting.'

'Perfect. I'd like to pop into the library too while we're here. Will there be enough time for that?'

'Take as much time as you need. As long as we're home in time to give Loki his dinner.' Harley climbed off the bike. 'He'll never forgive us if we're late.'

'Not when he takes his dish washing duties so seriously, no.'

He'd like to kiss her, but the hospital car park wasn't

the best place for it with half the town milling about, already giving them suspicious looks. No doubt they were expecting him to be as angry with her as they were with her father. It would take a while to convince the people of Wongan Creek that they could work together to overcome the crisis instead of working against each other.

He wasn't about to draw any more attention to her than she already had focused on herself. He settled for a quick, friendly pat on her shoulder and promised himself he'd steal that kiss later. 'Exactly.'

Tameka handed him her helmet. 'See you later then.'

'I'll be waiting.' And no doubt checking his watch every five minutes until she showed up and shared the results of her check-up and the fallout from the missing persons' report.

Tameka slipped into the police station with the good news that her burns were healing well, her pain meds dosage had been reduced, and the doctor was happy.

The library had proved a dead end in the search for answers to her flashback about Ryan. The old newspaper articles had told her nothing more than she already knew. Dad had locked the shed not knowing anyone was inside.

Maybe she had it wrong. Maybe Dad hadn't kicked her on his way out of the burning kitchen. Maybe in his haste to go for help, he'd tripped over her. But he hadn't gone for help. He'd disappeared. And she was making excuses for his behaviour again.

She ditched her plan to ask the sergeant about the shed fire in case she raised any unnecessary suspicions in the wake of her father's disappearance and the fallout from the spray drift.

'Good morning, Sergeant.'

'Ah, Tameka. How are you? Recovering well, I hope?'

'Yes, thank you.'

'Great. How can I help you today then? I'm about fifteen minutes away from doing an induction with my new recruit, so I'll have to hurry you along, I'm afraid.'

Doubt edged its way into her mind. Was reporting her father missing really necessary? What if he came back tonight or tomorrow or next week? He'd be furious with her for making a scene over nothing. Yet reporting it might give her a little protection from his anger.

'It's my father. I haven't seen him since the night of the fire.'

Riggs frowned. 'Yes, I wondered about that, but since there've been no reports about him going missing, I thought maybe he'd just gone away somewhere to avoid the fallout over this nonsense with the spray drift. Into the city or something. I've had my hands full around here with the unrest up at the mine site and

Harry's sheep going missing. Odd. So, he left … when exactly?'

Tameka shivered. What was the penalty for lying to a police officer? 'While I was preparing dinner.'

The sergeant pulled a form from the stack of trays on the counter. 'What state was he in? Had he been drinking? Did you argue? Was he angry when he left?'

When wasn't he angry? 'Same as always. He might have had a drink or two.' Or ten.

'Do you think he's in any danger?'

'I don't know. He took the ute and hasn't come back.'

'Has he disappeared like this before?'

Tameka shook her head. 'Not for this long at a time.'

Riggs looked her in the eye, and she struggled not to look away. 'Right, well I can put out an alert to be on the lookout for his ute. For now, we can list him as whereabouts unknown and start searching all the usual places like hospitals and shelters. Does he have a mobile phone?'

'Yes, but he doesn't use it often.' By now though, Dad could be anywhere. Halfway across the Nullarbor if the ute would get him that far, out of mobile range deep in the bush somewhere.

'We might be able to pick up a signal from it linked to the closest satellite. We'll do everything we can to find him, love.'

He pushed the paperwork forward and as she signed

her name, she swayed between hoping they did and wishing they wouldn't. 'Thank you.'

The door of the station opened, and a pretty young police officer stepped inside with a nervous smile. Riggs put the report in a file and stepped around the counter.

'My victim has arrived. I'll have to leave you now, Tameka, but I'll get our new recruit here onto it right after induction.'

'Thank you, Sergeant Riggs.' She smiled at the young police officer. 'Good luck and welcome to Wongan Creek.'

'Thanks.' She held out her hand. 'Constable Merryn Haines.'

Tameka's hand was squeezed in a tight grip. 'Tameka Chalmers.'

'Your first case, Haines. Missing person. A real one. Normally it's Harry Murchison's sheep we're looking for. A bit different out here from the city.'

'A lot quieter, I'm sure, Sarge.'

Riggs grinned. 'Don't bank on it.' He opened the door for Tameka and waved her through. 'I'll be in touch as soon as we have any news for you. You be careful if you're going to that meeting at the Town Hall. The boys are restless, and they might start an argument with you in the absence of your father. If anyone gives you any trouble you come to me, okay?'

'I'll be fine.'

Tameka stepped out into the sunshine and made her

way down to the Town Hall to the meeting. She searched the crowded room for Harley and found him in the fourth row from the front.

Quietly she slipped into the seat he'd saved for her as Tom Baker stepped up to the microphone and tried to still the rumblings and shouts.

Tameka's heart wedged in her throat as eyes shifted in her direction. They had every reason to be angry and Riggs was right. With her father nowhere to be seen, they'd hold her accountable. If what she thought had happened to Ryan was true, this hall full of people could turn into a lynch mob in an instant. The resentment already simmered. Her dad hadn't exactly made a good name for himself by being less than friendly.

Harley bent his head to hers and whispered, 'How did it go?'

She turned her gaze from the crowd to Harley, those blue eyes seeing right into her soul. 'All good. Doc's happy. Riggs reported Dad as whereabouts unknown but at no immediate risk of danger. He promised to let the other stations in the district know so they could keep an eye out for the ute.'

He took her hand and squeezed it tight. 'It's a start, Tikki.'

Yes, but the start of what? Another chapter of the nightmare that dogged her life? All the cash was missing from the safe, the bank account was all but empty, and her secret stash of silver coins wouldn't get her far. She couldn't even afford to run away.

She looked back at the stage as Tom began to talk despite the heckles from the crowd. Her heart warmed to him a little more as he steered the subject away from the blame game, clearly in her corner — something else she would be thankful for if she had to leave town. At least she'd had someone on her side.

Was this how they'd treat her and her father if the truth came out about how Ryan died? With anger and disrespect, ready to lay the blame with a whole family rather than at the feet of the person who'd committed the crime. No, it would be a lot worse because if what she'd seen was true, her father's crime would weigh much more heavily than hectares of damaged, useless crop. And even her allies would become enemies.

'I understand you're angry,' Tom said, holding up his hand for silence. 'But let's focus on how we can salvage what we have left.'

'There's nothing left to salvage,' Mal shouted from the front row. 'Where the hell is Chalmers? Did you invite him to this circus?'

'He's not here but his farm manager is,' someone else said. The sneer in the man's words gripped Tameka's stomach in its fist. 'Maybe his daughter should be made accountable. How many more years do we have to put up with this shit?'

Calls of agreement echoed through the hall.

Behind her, Harry stood. 'Oi! Cut it out, you mongrels. Mal, didn't I tell you to get your head out your arse? And you, Terry. You should know better. How long did it take you to stop using those same damn herbicides on your wheat?'

'That's not the point. The point is Louis Chalmers is still using them when everyone else has stopped. He needs to pay.' Terry clambered out into the aisle and made his way up to the fourth row. 'She needs to pay.'

Harry pushed him back with his cane. 'Pull your head in, man. Do you think the girl would have shown her face here today if she didn't care? She's lost her home, fresh out of hospital with burns to deal with. This is no bloody picnic for her either.'

Tameka wanted to curl up against Harley and pretend none of this was happening. She wanted to run from the hall and keep running as all eyes centred on her.

Harley stood. 'Please, Terry, sit down. Let's deal with this fairly and in an orderly way. The National Farmers Federation is here to help us sort something out. Let's not make this personal.'

Anger, red and ugly, leeched into the man's face, the thick chords in his neck standing out as he shouted, 'How can it not be fucking personal? I've lost an entire crop of greens. How the fuck am I supposed to feed my family when the bank is ready to seize my machinery because I can't pay for it anymore?' He pointed a finger at Tameka. 'And you … you just sit there like a pampered princess and say nothing. Just like your father who is too much of a coward to come in here and sort his shit out.'

'Sit down!' Harley stepped out of the row and towered over Terry.

Tameka's stomach churned. Pampered princess. If only they knew the truth, but there'd been enough violence, enough hurt, enough blame thrown around. She uncurled out of her seat and stood, dwarfed by the anger in the crowd, her heart aching for their loss, for her own and for the fact that no matter what she said, she was powerless to change a thing. She stepped in front of Terry and accepted the arm Harley placed around her shoulders.

'I'm sorry for your loss, Terry. I'm sorry everyone has suffered so badly this season. I can't promise miracles or change what's been done. All I can do is talk to him when he gets back. I have nothing to give in terms of compensation. I have nothing left and my father is missing.'

'The mongrel's done a runner?' Harry leaned forward.

'No. He's just … gone … away.'

The shouts died and the whispers dissipated. Harsh words clung to the lips of the crowd but didn't fall. Tameka swallowed the pain that clung to her throat, pushed her way between Harry and Terry and walked out, her mind barely registering Harley as he followed her.

People stepped aside to allow her to pass. She kept her head down and prayed the tears that stung her eyes wouldn't fall, that she wouldn't break apart in front of them and spill the truth about the horrors she'd lived with every day. And when she reached the steps, she took a deep breath, lifted her face to the wintery sun and bit down on the scream that blocked her throat.

Harley's arms slipped around her and drew her head under his chin, his hand cupping her head against his heart. She listened to the soothing beat until the tears slipped away and the numb emptiness inside her returned.

Chapter Eighteen

Sunday dawned bright and sunny, but a little chilly. Tameka snuggled into Harley's side and toed Loki from his spot on her feet. Leaving would be even harder after sharing Harley's bed, but she'd enjoy this false sense of security for as long as she could.

He stirred beside her, running a hand over his face to chase away sleep. 'How's your back feeling? Are we still going to the picnic today?'

Tameka stretched against him. 'When the town is ready to hang me in my father's absence? Do you think it's a good idea?'

A day out in the sunshine that didn't involve toiling the soil and worrying about how she'd ever get out of this hole sounded like good medicine, but there was no healing out there for her. She'd survived three trips into town and still there was no forgiveness for the Chalmers. Their existence had destroyed too many dreams. And damn it, she knew the effects of that too well.

Now the town knew she'd reported Dad missing too. He'd left just like Mum had. What kind of speculation would that churn up? Nothing she had an answer to, but she did have Harley.

'We don't have to if you don't want to.' Harley turned on his side to face her, pressing a kiss to her lips. 'I can find other ways to entertain you.'

And oh boy, could he. She smiled, her heart doing a little dance even though this Utopia would be short-lived. Especially with their future so uncertain. If things were different she'd marry Harley and live happily ever after, but that only happened in fairy tales.

'Tempting. It would be so easy to hide.'

'And let them win? You're stronger than that, Tikki.'

'Am I? What would the point of going be?' She tucked a hand under her cheek and held his gaze.

'You'll be proving you're the better person. Coming out in support of the community instead of staying hidden under a blanket. Not that I have a problem with you staying exactly where you are.' He grinned and let his hand explore freely under the covers.

'I guess you're right. This is something I can do for the community that I couldn't do if Dad was here. The Chalmers have done nothing to help the people of

Wongan Creek. It's time I changed that.' Even if it was only once. The CWA had helped her while she was in hospital, no questions asked, and nothing wanted in return. Heather had come forward and they'd formed a tentative friendship. Mr and Mrs Baker were clearly on her side. She could do this. 'And you'll be there to protect me. You and Harry.'

'That's my girl.' Harley kissed her long and well until her toes curled against his legs in satisfaction.

'Keep that up, Baker, and we won't be going anywhere.'

His deep, sexy, throaty chuckle against her ear almost had her melting into the mattress. 'Promises, promises.' His hand made contact with her backside in a light tap. 'Let's do this. We can spend the day in bed tomorrow.' He threw back the covers. 'Up, Your Laziness. I need to deal with that onesie.'

'Like you could spend the day in bed anyway,' she scoffed.

Somewhere in the middle of the night he'd been up and working in his study, his head likely full of ideas since the National Farmers Federation had proposed a rescue package that included various grants. He'd talked about it all through dinner, plotted out a section of land he could use for research and alternative, organic methods of weed control. His excitement was catching, and Tameka found herself wishing she could stay and help make his dreams come true.

The only dream for her had been the one about Ryan that had woken her at three in the morning with her heart pounding and a cold sweat trickling down her spine. The burning shed, her father padlocking the door and screams ringing in her head. Always the same memory, never differing from one dream to the next, but a timely reminder that her heart couldn't belong to Harley. Ever.

Should she tell him? If she did it would open old wounds on the anniversary of Ryan's death. If it was a skewed memory of what she'd seen that day, it would only cause him unnecessary heartache. And telling him would raise questions about how she came to remember details so long after the event.

Harley hovered over her, leaning on his elbow for support. 'Are you going to lie there and daydream all day?' He touched her forehead gently. 'What's put that frown on your face, Tikki?'

'Can we visit Ryan today?' She'd take flowers again like they used to. When as kids they used to sit at the edge of Ryan's grave and tell him all about their adventures. How they missed him being part of their lives. Back when life was all about discovery and less about being responsible grown-ups.

'I think he'd like that.'

'I do too.'

'We'll go there first and then on to the picnic, okay?'

Tameka smiled and tried to push away the sadness. 'Okay, but you need to move so I can get up.'

He leaned closer. 'One more kiss for the road.'

No point arguing when their kisses carried a time limit.

Liv Waterman's vineyard was teeming with people by the time Harley pulled into a parking spot. Music streamed out from the cellar door, and kids played happily on the colourful playground equipment while their parents tasted wine and liqueurs or drank coffee. Laughter pealed out across the lawns and gardens, a welcome change from the tense mood that had gripped the town since harvest.

Tameka got out of the ute with a blanket under her arm and waited for Harley to lift the picnic basket out of the back. She waved to Shirley who returned her greeting enthusiastically and came over.

'Hey, guys, glad you could make it. Tameka, sweetheart, I heard you reported your dad missing. Are you holding up okay? Is there anything we can do to help?'

Shirley's high energy always left Tameka exhausted. Today though even Harley's mum seemed a little preoccupied. Understandably so since they'd found fresh flowers on Ryan's grave that said his parents had already been to visit their eldest son.

'I'll be fine, thanks. I'm sure he'll be back soon. Maybe the ute broke down somewhere and he's stranded. And Dad has never been a fan of mobile phones, so I doubt he has his with him.'

Not that she'd found it anywhere in the house either, but any more elaboration would only raise more questions she didn't have answers to.

'I hope he's okay, sweetheart. I'm sure he will be.'

'He'll be fine.' Even though a small, selfish part of her wished he wasn't. Hoped that he wouldn't come back at all.

'Has he gone off like this before? I didn't think he left the farm very often.'

Tameka shifted on her feet. 'He doesn't normally, no.'

And so, the questions started. Shirley's heart was in the right place, but this would be one of the many times today she'd have to answer the same question and steer the town's curiosity away from the raw truth. Maybe coming to the picnic hadn't been such a good idea after all.

'You must be so worried.'

Worried he might come back, relieved that he hadn't yet and terrified for what would happen when he did. 'A little.'

'Well, it's lovely to see you here today, Tameka. Hopefully, the picnic will take your mind off things for a while. Will you be staying for most of the day?'

Harley stepped up beside her, the picnic basket in his hands. He set it down at his feet and placed a reassuring hand at Tameka's back. 'We'll see how it goes hey, Mum? I might have to take Tikki home if she gets tired. We don't want her overdoing it now that she's on the mend.'

'Of course, darling. I totally understand. I'll make sure she doesn't get caught up in anything too stressful.'

'Great. I'll leave her in your hands while I find Travis and Harry. I need to rub in the Eagles win over the Hawks last night and claim my five bucks.'

Tameka wanted to grab his arm and anchor him to her side because no-one understood her like Harley did. Shirley meant well, but she was no protection against inquisitive minds and prying eyes.

Harley gave her hip a rub. 'I'll be back soon.'

She cursed herself for having become so reliant on his strength and support again. How easily she'd fallen under his spell and rekindled their friendship along with the flame of attraction. As if the eight years they'd been apart had simply melted away.

But then the separation had been her father's doing. He'd insisted she have nothing to do with the Bakers, threatened that if she did, he'd make her regret it. And because she knew he was capable of making her regret it in the most painful way possible, she'd obeyed.

She'd put her head down and bum up and tried her best to make up for her sins by working hard, only to learn she'd sacrificed everything for a father who would never be happy no matter what she did. And now the damage was done.

After today she'd have to rebuild her wall brick by brick, or she'd be leaving more than a little piece of herself behind if she left.

Shirley smiled knowingly at them, some of her sadness slipping away as she watched them standing close together. Tameka would have to burst her bubble the moment they were alone. She couldn't have Harley's mum building her hopes up only to have them blown up and destroyed in the days to come. The Bakers had enough to deal with.

As Harley walked away, Shirley linked her arm through Tameka's. 'Come along, sweetheart. The CWA ladies are keen to see how you're healing up.'

Maybe the physical scars were but the mental scars kept being ripped open until they bled again, she thought as they walked across the park.

The ladies had set up a workstation under the shade of a canopy amidst chatter and laughter. They were met with a chorus of greetings and warm hugs, and not one single question, thank God. Before she could escape, she found herself buttering buns and peeling onions for the sausage sizzle, enjoying their company shoulder to shoulder with her new friend, Heather. She hadn't realised how much she would enjoy it or how much she'd missed out on during her father's self-imposed exile.

And when sunset rolled around, her feet were tired, her mind exhausted and she almost felt … happy. Tameka slipped her hand into Harley's as he stood talking to Travis and Harry, their laughter and teasing easy in the dimming light as they talked football, farming methods and the future of Wongan Creek.

As his fingers closed around hers, enveloping them in warmth, she could dream that this happiness would last, and the nightmare of tomorrow wouldn't come.

Chapter Nineteen

With the picnic a pleasant memory she'd taken away with her and reality kicking in, Tameka stood back to admire the new shoots, bright green against the rich, dark soil. Still no news on her father, but that didn't mean she could stand idle until he decided to show up. Or not.

She checked her watch and shrugged off the burn from the still raw patches on her back. Why hadn't the pump started? By now the drip-feeders should be leaking water into the rows at a slow and steady pace. Damn it, please don't let the pump have packed up too. Hadn't she spent enough time today with a wrench in her hand?

If only Dad had listened to her and upgraded to the solar-powered surface pump instead of the archaic siphon version they couldn't even get spare parts for.

Resigned to yet another patch-up job, she slipped a screwdriver, wrench and can of silicone spray into her pockets. Just what she needed when she'd planned to have everything watered before midday kicked in. Turning from the crop, she took the service path between the two fields down the slope to the dam.

On the bank, the weeping willow dipped its branches into the water. The flattened grass around the dam indicated they'd had visitors in the night. Roos most likely, judging from the droppings.

She'd have to find a way to deal with them before they sank their teeth into her juicy new crop. If she could lure them back across the creek into the national park that bordered The Cranky Lizard vineyard, they'd have plenty of natural bush to nibble on and loads of shady cover.

In the early morning light, the sun sparkled off the surface of the dam, bright and cheerful. Tameka dropped her sunnies down from her head onto her nose to cut the glare. Normally this spot brought peace and tranquillity. Today it brought annoyance and yet another temporary repair.

To her left, the pump laboured in the silence of the morning. So, it wasn't the pump that had failed then. She sighed. That would have been the easy fix. Now she'd have to find out what was stopping it from pumping water out of the dam and into the irrigation pipes.

She moved to hit the emergency stop button on the top of the housing and listened to the instant silence that fell across the dam. In the trees that lined the west side of the water, a kookaburra laughed and was answered by the squawk of the cockatoos.

Irritation skittered along her nerve endings. The way her luck was running there'd be a blockage at the intake which was about four metres deep under the ice-cold water. She wasn't exactly equipped to go diving into the dam in wintery conditions today. Not that she'd be able to anyway because of her burns.

Even if she could, the thought of diving to the bottom of the murky water to unblock the intake set her imagination running wild. Alone, she couldn't risk becoming entangled in the mud and water grass at the bottom.

To her right, a flimsy-looking object floated towards the bank. Damn it, had more debris blown out of the remains of the homestead and found its way into the dam? How many more times did she have to pull scorched junk out of the water while she fought with the insurance company over the payments in arrears?

She moved closer, looking around for a stick long enough to fish out whatever it was. God knew what else had found its way into the dam and clogged up the pump intake.

Finding a long, thin broken branch, Tameka edged her way towards the rubbish. Not plastic or anything that resembled something out of the remains of the kitchen, but rather something out of the laundry. Muddy brown material. Like a shirt maybe.

Her breath hitched in her throat. *Oh God, Dad.* Was this how her father had chosen to end his misery? What colour shirt had he been wearing the night of the fire? Blue and yellow-checked flannel, worn and faded.

No, not Dad. There was nothing weighing the material down, no-one attached to the tattered piece that drifted on the surface of the water.

Relief mixed with regret flooded her. How was it possible she could wish him dead and alive at the same time? She edged closer still and pulled the material closer with the stick, the water lapping at her boots.

The pattern. *Oh God no.* Something soft, cheerfully floral, once full of colour before it had been stained brown. *Oh Jesus!* The material caught on the roots of the weeping willow. *No. Please God, no.* The last time she'd seen that dress …

Forcing her feet to move, she edged away. Her heart pounded, tears stung her eyes. She blinked them back. It couldn't be.

Her gaze fell on yellow-brown stained shapes wedged in the muddy feet of the tree, perfectly curved—like a bone with rounded edges that might fit into a joint socket. A few smaller ones scattered nearby.

Please let them belong to a roo. But as she looked more closely, doubt edged around the fringes of fear.

There was no mistaking where she'd seen that pattern on a dress before and the bones were too delicate to belong to a roo.

'No!' Her cry chased the birds from the trees around her. She slapped her hands to her mouth, nausea rising in her stomach. 'No.'

Slipping to the ground on her knees, Tameka struggled to focus her thoughts on what she'd seen that awful day. Mum standing behind Dad, her hands pressed against her throat as he hauled Harley out of the ute.

The floral cotton swirling around her legs, hanging from her delicate frame as she ran up behind him. Mum crying, begging Dad to stop as he dragged Tameka home, his grip on her arm tight and rough with anger. The pink floppy hat she'd worn to protect her skin from the harsh sun hanging from a string down her mum's back.

Her father's words, angry and loud as they echoed through the house and the locked door of her bedroom. *If you leave, Mai, you're never coming back.*

No. The word echoed through her mind. There had to be a logical explanation. Not the one forming in her mind. Had Mum fallen into the dam? Unlikely. Too far from the road she would've had to take. Dad's rage. The bonfire. His two-day drinking binge after Mum left.

Tameka's hand shook as she stood and pulled her phone from her pocket. Signal. Thank God there was a signal here. She dialled the number for the police station, praying Sergeant Riggs was in and not out on the road somewhere. If not, she'd have to call triple zero instead. No, not even triple zero. That was for emergencies. This had gone beyond that point.

'Wongan Creek Station, Riggs speaking.'

'Sergeant Riggs.' *Oh, God.* 'It's Tameka Chalmers out at Golden Acres.'

'Hey, Tameka. How can I help? Has your father come back?'

Tameka's hands shook as she gripped the phone to her ear in one hand while the other clung to the stick, her knuckles white, the wood biting into her palm. She'd been fine until she'd heard the policeman's voice. Until the shock of her find tore the memories from their place locked in her heart.

'You'll need to come. Please.' A sob rose in her throat. She swallowed around it. 'There are … bones. I've found bones. And a dress. Mum's dress. I'm sure it's hers …'

Not even sure she was making sense, Tameka backed away from the tree, her boots clinging to the mud, her thoughts irrational and scattered as she tried to make sense of finding her mother's dress in the dam.

If Dad was somewhere out there in the bush would he see the cop cars rolling up the access road? Would he come back and pretend he didn't know about the fire? Would he be surprised that she'd survived it? And what would he make of her mother's dress in the dam?

There'd be an investigation. He'd be angry she didn't come to him first. But how could she when she didn't know where he bloody was? Would he even care after he'd walked away from the burning house with her inside, unconscious?

Was that how Mum had ended up in the dam? Nausea rose in her throat, but she forced it down as Riggs' voice echoed in her ear.

'A dress? Bones? Hang in there, young lady. Don't touch a thing. I'll come over right away.'

Hysteria rose in her throat, fear curled around it. She was staring at what could be her mother's remains. The danger had passed eight years ago. 'Please, come quickly.'

Tameka's lime green beanie disappeared into the reeds around the dam. So far today, Harley had seen her take a wrench to the tractor and a crowbar to the seeder and it wasn't even eight o' clock yet. Now it looked like the pump on the dam was giving her trouble. Next to him, Loki nudged his hand and Harley delivered a quick ear rub.

He understood her need for independence, to get on with the job of taking care of her father's farm. He'd offered to help, but she'd declined. That didn't mean he couldn't keep a close eye on things while he went about his own chores.

Since the day of the picnic, his gut had coiled around the feeling something awful was about to happen. As if it could possibly get any worse. Fires, punch-ups, flared tempers, the farmers calling an intervention from the National Farmers' Federation — it wasn't exactly all good news and cheerful tidings.

The cockatoos launched into flight from the trees on the dam's west bank and Loki lost it to give chase. He launched through the gate and streaked off down the service lane on the Chalmers property.

'Loki, heel!'

The dog ignored his command, his bark reverberating through the otherwise quiet morning air as he streaked off down to where Harley had seen Tameka in the reeds.

'Damn it.' He prayed nothing had happened to Tameka. If she'd slipped into that ice-cold, muddy water she risked infection in the burns that had begun to heal so well. Or if she'd fallen on her back and grazed them open again …

Harley broke into a jog and chased Loki down to the dam, the unease coiled in his stomach tightening to a knot. He reached her out of breath, the ice-cold air burning in his lungs.

Tameka sat in the mud at the edge of the water next to the willow tree, her knees hugged to her chest, sunnies dangling between them, her body shaking and her phone lying at her feet in the mud.

What the hell? Loki made a beeline for her, nudging at her with his nose. She lifted her face. Tears streaked the dirt smeared on her cheeks. His heart rose in his throat. The bad feeling in his gut clenched at his abs.

'Loki, heel.' He crouched down as Loki ignored his instruction and leaned against her instead. 'Hey, what's up? Pump packed it in?'

Maybe the pump had been the last straw for her today. Even in the days when they'd shared the dam, it had played up regularly. And with everything else that had happened to her these last few weeks, perhaps this was the final nail in the cross she'd tried to carry alone for so long.

Tameka shook her head, but no words came as she tucked her sunnies into her jacket pocket and pulled her beanie from her head. Her short dark hair stuck up haphazardly where she fisted her fingers into it, her normally healthy olive complexion grey under the streaks of dirt and grease. Clearly, it hadn't been an easy morning.

She opened her mouth to speak but her face crumpled, and her bottom lip quivered. Twice now he'd seen her crumble like this, and he didn't like it. Not a bit. Not when it broke his heart to see her this way.

'Oh, Tikki.' Harley parked his butt in the mud next to her and gathered her in his lap, tugging a little harder when she resisted before giving in. 'What's happened, baby?'

Nothing. No response, except for the sobs that shook her body.

He tightened his arms around her, tucked her head under his chin and looked over at the weeping willow that held so many happy memories for them.

Harley narrowed his eyes. A tattered lump of discoloured material moved with each lap of the current but stayed stuck on a root without floating away.

The knot in his stomach tightened. He knew that dress. He'd caught a brief sight of it behind Tikki's dad as he'd hauled Harley out of the ute by the scruff of his neck. Her mum's cry of 'Stop!' as old man Chalmers raised his fist. *Jesus*. Loki settled against his thigh, leaning in close with a little whine.

'Is that what I think it is stuck in the tree roots?'

Tameka nodded against his chest, her fists bunching on his jacket.

'I'm so sorry, Tikki.'

He squeezed her closer, his hand cupping her head, his heart aching for her. Maybe Mai had thrown her suitcase in the dam before she left. Not that it would make any sense for her to do that. But then nothing about Tameka's situation in the years they'd been apart made sense. He hoped with all his heart it was just Mai Chalmers' clothes in the water and that the dam didn't hold any other secrets.

'Bones too.' Her whisper feathered against his throat, tears wet on his skin. 'I've been down here a hundred times … never saw it before.'

Jesus, bones? Where the hell had they come from? Had her mum's remains been dragged out of the bush? There'd been an increase in dingoes getting past the dog fence two hundred kilometres to the east. Had they ranged this far down?

That would mean Mai Chalmers had wandered into the bushland surrounding the farms and got lost, a perfectly good explanation for why she hadn't returned. Either that or she'd been in the water all this time. He didn't want to think about how she got there, but his imagination took him on the journey anyway.

Louis Chalmers hadn't reported his wife's disappearance. He'd allowed the people of Wongan Creek to assume she'd left him and her daughter, walked away from the farm into the unknown at the edge of their outback town.

Pieces of the puzzle that was Mai's disappearance dropped into place and he didn't like the picture. Old man Chalmers' rampage, cutting the Bakers' supply to the dam. He was an arsehole, but would he really have murdered his wife and dumped her in the dam?

Leaping to conclusions again, Baker. With the house on Bakers Hill so close to the dam, surely they would have seen or heard something if he had? Harley cast his mind back to the night Mai Chalmers left. No, he'd seen nothing because he'd gone home to tell Mum and Dad, to talk through what happened before he'd slammed his bedroom door and punched his anger and frustration into his pillow at putting Tameka in the position he had.

'Have you called the cops?'

Tameka nodded.

'Good. Hang in there, baby. We'll get answers soon.' He hoped they were ones that wouldn't cause anyone more pain, but the sinking feeling in his gut said they would.

What the hell was happening to this town? The bloody place was unravelling at the seams. It felt like one disaster rolled in on the heels of another.

The ominous click of a rifle echoed in his ears, chased by a low snarl from Loki as he leapt to his feet on full alert. But it was the almost inhuman growl Harley recognised as his heart clenched with dread.

'Get your filthy fucking hands off my daughter.'

The underlying threat in Louis Chalmers' voice sent shockwaves fizzing through Harley's blood. *Holy fuck.* He straightened his spine against the cold fear that crawled up it. If Louis knew what had happened to his wife … if he'd thrown her in the dam … Jesus, he and Tameka could be in deep shit.

'I'm letting go. You don't need the gun.' He moved slowly, releasing his hold on Tameka, debating over talking him into putting the gun down, but Louis Chalmers had gone beyond the edge of reason.

'One move, Baker. One move and I'll blow your fucking head off like I should have done years ago.' His voice rose, ringing out across the water, making Loki snap and snarl. 'Get the fuck up here, girl. You're a no-good slut just like your mother was.'

Harley gripped Loki's collar to stop the dog from leaping at Chalmers and felt the wrench of muscles as the dog pulled against his hold. He didn't want Chalmers shooting his dog … shooting anyone … but God help him, if her father insulted Tameka one more time, he'd face the consequences and ram his fist down Louis Chalmers' throat.

'Dad …'

Tameka scrambled off Harley's lap onto her feet, her hands outstretched. Loki growled deep in his throat and went into stalk mode, hackles raised, teeth bared.

'Call that fucking mongrel off and get up.'

'Down, Loki. Down.'

Loki obeyed, but the dog's sides quivered with the suppressed need to attack as Harley rose slowly to his feet. Any sudden movement could set Chalmers off and there'd been enough bloodshed on Golden Acres.

Harley moved Tameka behind him and got a good look at the older man. Louis Chalmers looked like he'd been dragged through the bush backwards. His face was grimy and unshaven, his clothes dirty, wrinkled, and smelly. Wherever he'd been there weren't any ablution facilities, and it didn't look like he'd taken a change of wardrobe.

But it was the sheer craziness in his bloodshot eyes that had Harley's grip on Tameka tightening and his tongue clamping down on everything he'd like to say to the cold bastard. The tension mounted in his gut. Louis' hands were shaking, and the rifle was pointed right at Harley's head.

'I can explain.'

'Think I'm interested in your excuses, Baker? You're an interfering pain in the arse and you should be dead like your brother. That little shit got what he deserved intruding in my shed. And here you are, trespassing on my land, pawing at my daughter again like the filthy animal you are.'

The comment about Ryan had anger rising in Harley's throat. And where had the old bastard been while his daughter lay injured in hospital, in excruciating pain, with burns to her back? When, even now, the worst of those burns still hurt. He had no bloody right to be so territorial about her or his land when he'd deserted both. Tameka shifted against Harley's hold.

'Don't move, Tikki. For God's sake, stay behind me.'

'No, Harley, this has gone on long enough. I want answers. Dad, put the rifle down.' Tameka's voice was scratchy as she moved from behind Harley to stand at his side. 'You need to know the police are coming. Please, we don't need any more trouble. Don't let them find you with a loaded rifle.'

Louis swayed on his feet and the whiff of stale whisky hit Harley in the nose as he bellowed, 'What the bloody hell did you call the police for?'

'I had to. I think I've found Mum. *Look*, Dad.'

Tameka pointed towards the dress where it fluttered in the water as if Mai Chalmers would rise at any moment. Harley shivered. Louis Chalmers stared at the tree, his bloodshot eyes wide, his skin so pale the broken purple veins on his cheeks, drawn by years of drinking, stood out against his cheeks. Loki barked as the white four-wheel drive police wagon rumbled down the service road, throwing up red dust in its wake.

Chapter Twenty

Harley kept an eye on the wavering rifle as Sergeant Riggs stepped out of the police wagon, his newly sworn-in police constable, Merryn Haines, not far behind him.

Harley shivered. Another body, another life gone. How many more secrets lay buried between the creek and the hills?

'Put that bloody rifle down, Chalmers. Haines, take that thing off him. I've got a thumping headache and a bloody lynch mob looking for you to deal with yet. I don't need a God damn shooting on my hands too. What's this about bones?'

Constable Merryn Haines stepped up beside him, notebook in hand, her eyes on Louis' rifle. 'Please put the safety on that rifle, sir, and slowly place it on the ground.'

Outnumbered, Louis obeyed, his movements automatic albeit reluctant. He kept it in his hand ignoring the constable's request to lay it down on the ground.

'I've put the bloody safety on, that's enough. I'm not about to shoot anyone, you stupid girl. Not with fucking cops as witnesses.'

'That's not what it looked like when we arrived, and you had these two held at gunpoint. And now I'll have to fill out a report for the misuse of a firearm. I've got enough bloody paperwork to do with you being reported missing and then showing up again alive and ...' Sergeant Riggs rubbed his forehead and sniffed. 'Let's just go with *alive*, hey. I don't want to have to file a separate report because you've insulted an officer of the law.'

'Not much of a bloody police force if you're letting women in to do a man's job.' His eyes trailed to Tameka, hatred burning brightly in them as he sneered at his daughter, anger making his shoulders stiff and his hands clench around the butt of the rifle. 'Burnt the fucking house down while I was away, I see. Useless, absolutely bloody useless. Just like her fucking mother.'

The rage Harley had seen in the man earlier had intensified the moment he'd spotted Mai's dress. Had he been waiting all these years to find out what happened to his wife, or did he already know?

And raising the issue of the fire now in the presence

of police, was he trying to clear himself of any blame? Exactly the type of dick thing Louis Chalmers would do.

Tameka stiffened against him before she stepped out of Harley's hold, squared her shoulders, and slipped on her sunglasses. 'The bones I found are over there under the willow tree. Lodged in the roots. The dress ... it's the one Mum was wearing the day she left.'

Sergeant Riggs frowned. 'Right. I'll go take a look at it then. Chalmers, hand over that rifle now or I'll cuff you. Understood?'

'Do I look like a fucking moron?'

Merryn stepped forward and took the gun out of Louis' reluctant hands. 'I'll secure the weapon and get the tape from the car, Sarge. Cordon off the area.'

'Yes, do that, Haines.' He turned to Louis. 'Maybe you should come with me to identify the dress.'

Louis shook his head, his eyes darting away from the willow tree. 'I've got no interest in how that stupid bitch ended up in my dam. Serves her bloody right if she drowned. I wouldn't even know what she was fucking wearing when she left.'

Harley kept his eye on Chalmers. Where the hell had he been when his wife walked out the door that day, leaving her daughter behind? There were so many questions in his head since the fire.

Unease twisted up his spine, cementing his suspicions that Louis was involved in Mai's disappearance, a sixth sense dredging up a few of the unpleasant memories of their childhood as neighbours. Chalmers' uncontrolled anger triggered by the slightest thing. Mai visiting his mum with her jacket zipped up to her throat even in the heat of summer.

Merryn retrieved the blue and white police tape while the sergeant studied the bones and discoloured dress. Riggs prodded at yet another yellow-brown stained object with a stick as it drifted towards the edge, drawing it up onto the muddy bank. His flushed features paled. 'Haines!'

'Sir?'

'Contact Crime squad. We'll need forensics and a dive team.' Riggs stepped away from the bank. 'Tape across the entrance to the farm. No-one in, no-one out. Chalmers, it will take a few hours for them to get here. I'll need to ask you some questions in the meantime.'

'You can ask as many questions as you damn well like, but I don't have a clue as to how the bitch ended up in the water.'

Harley wanted to grab the man by the throat and shake him. As a kid he'd been terrified of Chalmers and his temper. No more. Because here stood a man who'd abandoned his daughter and had no respect for the living or the dead.

A real dad — a normal dad who loved his family — would have laid down his gun and come across to comfort his daughter. He'd seen the burnt-out homestead, yet he had no questions about it, only accusations.

Tameka's reluctance to discuss the events leading up to the fire. Ryan dying in old man Chalmers' shed. Her mum's remains in the dam. Jesus, he hoped the picture his mind was putting together was wrong, but it explained why she'd kept her distance from him for so long, hadn't let him see what was really happening on Golden Acres. God knew what she'd suffered at the hands of her father. It chilled him to the bone just thinking about it.

He reached for her hand, laced his fingers through her freezing cold, stiff ones. She turned into his side and Harley held her close while the sergeant questioned her father.

If the old man didn't like him holding her, he could damn well stuff it where the sun didn't shine. Because if he so much as looked at Tameka in the wrong way again, Harley would have no hesitation in taking Louis Chalmers down and teaching him a lesson. But violence didn't work on cruel men like her father, so Harley prayed the law would do the job for him.

'Chalmers.' Sergeant Riggs pulled out his notebook. 'Can you recall the events following your wife's departure from your home?'

'Why don't you ask Mai's offspring why her mother left? What she was doing that made her mother walk. Bringing shame on the family name by screwing around in the front seat of Harley Baker's ute. A whore just like her mother.'

Sergeant Riggs adjusted the hat on his head and stabbed the notebook with the tip of his pencil. 'Right now, I'm more interested in your version of events.'

'Typical bloody coppers. Always ready to lay the blame where it isn't due.'

'No-one's blaming anyone, Chalmers. We're fact-finding. It's what we do. You can answer my questions now or you can wait for the detectives to arrive.'

'How the bloody hell would I know? Maybe she jumped in, decided to finish off her own useless damn self.' Chalmers spat on the ground.

Tameka stiffened against Harley, and he rubbed her shoulder. He hated that she had to go through this.

Riggs squared his shoulders. 'Did you argue with your wife the day she left?'

'Well of course I argued with her. She had no control over her bloody daughter who should have been focusing on the job instead of spreading her legs.'

Anger surged through Harley. He released his hold on Tameka and stepped forward, hands raised to grab hold of Louis' filthy collar and shake the man for his disrespect. Loki growled and snarled.

'Stand down, Baker,' Riggs warned. 'And keep control of that dog.'

Tameka's hand closed around his arm. 'It's okay, Harley.'

It was far from okay, but Harley stepped back and let Riggs do his job.

'What happened after you argued with your wife?'

Chalmers glared at Tameka. 'I taught both the bitches a lesson they'd never forget. Then I packed Mai's suitcase and threw her out the door.'

Sickened by what he was hearing, Harley looked at Tameka. She didn't meet his gaze. Instead, she stared at her boots and his heart ached with the same pain her father had put her through.

'Did you take her anywhere? To the train station, a bus stop?'

'No, but I followed the bitch down the road to make sure she didn't come back.'

'Did you go anywhere near the dam with her that day?' Sergeant Riggs made a note in his book.

Louis looked at Tameka again, his face triumphant as if he'd won a prize. 'Unless I'm under arrest, I refuse to answer any further questions until the detectives arrive and I have a lawyer present.'

Riggs snapped his notebook shut and pulled the cuffs from his equipment belt, his professional mask slipping just a little to reveal the irritation and disgust behind it. 'Fine. Louis Chalmers, I am taking you into custody for questioning with regards to the unlawful use of a firearm endangering lives. Hands behind your back.' He snapped on the cuffs and walked him towards the wagon. 'I'll take you into town with me so we can get you cleaned up. The station has perfectly good shower facilities you can use.'

'Nothing but a trumped-up bloody charge.' Louis threw a mean look over at Tameka and Harley as the sergeant put a hand on his head to help him into the back seat of the wagon. 'Wait. One last thing for you to think about, girl. You know why you'll never inherit Golden Acres? Because you're not my daughter. You're the daughter of a whore. I wouldn't have a fucking clue who your father is. Your mother was pregnant when I met her. I thought she was having a son.'

Tameka clamped a fist to her mouth and her shoulders shook, but her spine stayed straight, and Harley wished she hadn't had to face the truth. Not that Louis Grade-A-Arsehole Chalmers deserved a daughter like the one he had, step or otherwise.

Harley's hands itched to reach for Louis's throat and choke him until he never uttered a word again, but that wouldn't help Tikki.

Riggs muttered something under his breath as he pushed Louis into the wagon a little more roughly than expected. Harley tightened his hold on Tameka and vowed to make sure Louis Chalmers never came within shooting distance of her again.

Chapter Twenty-One

The police dive team and forensics arrived at the same time the news of the discovery hit town and people began laying floral tributes at the gate. Sergeant Riggs made his statement to the press, a small matter of community interest added to the growing reports of damaged crops, farmers facing financial ruin and John Bannister's land grab.

She'd spent most of the afternoon and evening of the previous day at Wongan Creek's police station answering questions and lifting the lid on the Chalmers' box of secrets while Harley and Loki had waited patiently to take her home.

Tameka's back ached from the hard chairs and the burns still healing over, the happiness she'd found for such a short while scattered like her mother's bones, and accusations and threats from the man she'd always thought was her father echoing in her head. She'd stayed all this time for nothing.

She and Harley had hardly slept despite his weird concoction of hot chocolate and chamomile tea. They'd barely even spoken, neither sure of what to say, the whole crazy situation in limbo until the police recovered what answers they could from the dam.

Now, in the cold early morning, Harley's arm came around her shoulders as she watched the sun rise over the dam and the dive team gather their equipment in preparation for the depths of the ice-cold water.

She shivered against him. Louis had spent the night at the station, and she was glad about that. His threat rang in her ears, a promise that he wasn't done with her yet.

Having to tell the police everything had left her full of regret, without room even for the humiliation of having allowed herself to be controlled by him the way she had been.

Merryn Haines had understood. The police dealt with victims of domestic violence every day. They accepted the psychological reasons wives and children couldn't leave, couldn't talk to anyone who wouldn't understand unless they were victims themselves.

The police never asked that question a victim couldn't explain — why didn't you leave? — even when perhaps they didn't quite understand it themselves.

She'd seen the candles, letters and flowers left at the

gate to Golden Acres in memory of Mai as Harley had driven past it last night on the way to Bakers Hill from the police station.

Thankfully, the crowd had been kept from the scene, detained outside the gates. She couldn't handle the mix of gossip and sympathy, the speculation when truth and lies collided. There'd be enough of that to deal with later.

She accepted the thermal mug of tea Harley pushed into her gloved hand and sipped the hot, strong, sweet brew. Let him wrap his scarf around her neck and tug a beanie onto her head.

She'd come down before him, unable to settle, her mind churning on the possibilities of what had happened the night her father had followed her mother out the door. Before he'd returned to destroy almost everything in the house.

She didn't want to believe he was capable of murder, but she'd seen the madness for herself. With Ryan. As he'd stepped over her in the burning kitchen and left her to the mercy of the flames.

Maybe Mum had simply fallen into the water, unable to swim, too cold and weak to pull herself out. Maybe she'd become entangled in the water grass. But logic defied the reasoning. If she'd fallen in, she would have floated to the surface long before now.

The pump Tameka used every day, the water that fed the crops, the dam tainted with her mother's blood —

surreal, numbing. The first two divers went into the water.

'Come back up to the house, Tikki. You don't have to be here for this.'

'I do. I need to see, to process, to understand. Everyone thought she'd abandoned us. Even me. But she was here, all the time.'

Constable Haines came over with a blanket in her hands. 'If you're going to stay, you'll need to keep warm.' She draped it around Tameka's shoulders.

'Thanks.' Tameka clutched the edges of the blanket together with her free hand.

'Mum is coming over later with a few of the ladies from the CWA to prepare hot meals and drinks for the team,' Harley informed the young constable.

'They'll appreciate that. The water is freezing, and that breeze is a little chilly. Cuts right through you.' She tipped her head as Sergeant Riggs called her back inside the taped-off area. 'I've got to get back. It might be a while before they find something, Tameka. I can give you a call if you want to wait at Harley's?'

'Thank you. I'm fine here.' She owed it to her mum to stay, to see this through to the end or there'd never be a way forward.

'No worries.' With a little wave, Merryn Haines ducked back under the police tape.

'Any sign of Louis?' Harley sat down on the grass and

tugged Tameka down onto his lap where his body protected hers from the wind. They watched the movement in and out of the water as the divers coordinated their search.

She shivered against his question. 'No. He might still be with the police. A couple of detectives arrived from Perth late last night.'

'He chose a good time to come back.'

She couldn't ignore the irony in Harley's words. 'Or the worst time.'

He rested his cheek against her hair. 'Did he say where he's been for almost two weeks?'

Tameka shook her head, leaned back against him, and closed her eyes. 'I don't know what he's told the police. He hasn't spoken to me again.'

Not a bad thing, really. She wasn't sure she wanted to know what he'd been doing or where he'd been hiding. Especially not now. All she wanted was closure. And justice for Mum.

A flurry of movement and shouts dragged her attention back to the dam. She pulled out of Harley's arms and stood. 'They've found something.'

Two divers hauled a suitcase towards the shore, struggling to keep the lid closed and the contents from spilling out. The rest of the team entered the water to assist. Tameka ran with Harley close behind her, stopping at the taped-off area where they watched the suitcase being lifted from the dam.

'Mum's suitcase.' She covered her mouth with her hand.

Years of being in the mud and water had turned the once hard plastic mustard-coloured case rusty brown. One of the forensics team donned a pair of rubber gloves as they placed it on the table they'd set up on the grassy bank. He reached for the lid to open it, the locks almost rusted away.

'Jesus!' Sergeant Riggs covered his mouth and nose with his sleeve. 'Haines! Get the detectives down here now. And tell them to make sure Louis Chalmers is detained in custody.'

Tameka gagged as the wind picked up the stench of stale liquid, bacteria and a muddy soup of human remains. A bent and broken delicate skeleton, the bones stained yellow brown, rested in the case with the rusty, petrol-powered chainsaw used to weigh it down.

'No!' She turned and reached blindly for Harley, felt herself clamped against his chest, his hand holding her head to stop her from looking any closer.

'Tikki, I'm so sorry.'

She squeezed her eyes shut, trying to block out what she'd seen, but the image remained burned into her memory. The voices of the dive team reached her ears. She heard words like airtight, mummification and slower decomposition spoken as if what they were examining had not once been human. A mother. A wife.

A wife her father had carved up with his chainsaw

and shoved into a suitcase like the monster he was. It could only have been him. It explained everything about his behaviour since her disappearance. Why she hadn't taken Tameka with her.

It burned into her mind as surely as the fire that had taken Ryan after her father had padlocked the shed door. As surely as he'd left her to die then come back to make certain she had.

She let herself fall apart. She'd earned the right. She'd cheated death. She'd watch her father face justice for his crimes, and when the town turned on her for being Louis Chalmers' daughter, she'd leave.

But for now, for this one last time, she was in Harley's arms, crushed against his heart as he carried her home to Bakers Hill while she cried against his shoulder.

Chapter Twenty-Two

'How is she, love?' Mum placed a mug of hot, sweet tea on the table in front of Harley.

'Resting. With Loki.' He'd left her huddled around his dog, lying on her side staring blankly at the wall, his heart aching as she closed him out.

'The poor girl. Who would ever have imagined it, hey? At least we know Mai didn't walk out and leave her. That will be a comfort to her when the shock wears off.'

Harley hoped with all his soul that it would be. God knew she needed some comfort. By this afternoon, the news would be out and what couldn't yet be confirmed by police would be speculated upon and circulated anyway.

His dad appeared in the kitchen doorway followed

by Sergeant Riggs, who looked like he needed a drink. Harley didn't blame him at all. He could do with a stiff shot himself.

'I realise this is a difficult time, but I'll need to ask Tameka a few questions.'

'Is it really necessary, Riggs? Can't it wait a little longer?' Dad put a hand on the sergeant's shoulder.

'I wish it could, trust me. What the hell is happening in this town? It's like we're falling apart.' He played with the broad brim of his police-issue hat. 'What kind of man murders his wife and dumps her body in the dam? I'll never understand it, Tom. Never.'

Harley ran a hand through his hair. 'Kinda explains why he didn't want us using the dam after Mai left.' Surreal. Numbing. The thought of Tameka's mum discarded in such a cruel, uncaring way by a man who clearly had no heart, ate at his soul. That Tikki had lived with a murderer all this time … Jesus, that was hard to take.

Sergeant Riggs nodded. 'Yep, makes sense. Look, off the record until it becomes public knowledge, okay? The suitcase was lodged in the mud near the pump outlet. The boys think that with all the action the dam has seen lately because of the fire, the draw on the water dragged the suitcase out. Because the locks had rusted, it released some of the lighter items during movement. All that weighed it down was the chainsaw and years of mud.'

Tom shook his head. 'So, if it wasn't for the fire at the homestead, poor Mai might never have been found.'

The fire. Harley rubbed a hand over his face. Ironic that the fire that could have killed Tameka was the catalyst for releasing the dam's secret. 'Will you be asking Chalmers about the fire too? Where he's been since?'

Sergeant Riggs shrugged. 'Tameka pretty much claimed responsibility for the fire. A cooking accident.'

'With a fire blanket and extinguisher within easy reach? It doesn't make sense, Sarge.' Harley twisted the mug in his hands.

'She had a pretty nasty bump on the head, and you found her semi-conscious on the floor. I have no reason to believe it was anything other than the accident Tameka says it was.'

'Then I'll give you a reason.' Tameka's voice was quiet from the doorway, Loki by her side, but her words fell like rocks in the room. 'The fire was an accident, but it wasn't my fault. After this … I'm done protecting him.'

Harley stood and held out his hand to her. He hated seeing her so pale and drawn, her eyes empty as if her soul had been ripped out. Maybe it had.

Sergeant Riggs placed his hands on his hips. 'You're aware of the consequences of a false testimony, right?'

'Not a false testimony. Omission of facts.' She

placed her hand in Harley's, her fingers gripping his tightly.

'Do you want to do this down at the station?'

'No, I'll do it here because there is something else you need to know. That the Bakers need to know. About Ryan.'

Harley's heart crashed to the pit of his stomach, the sense of impending doom he'd had since the picnic blooming to nuclear proportions. A part of him didn't want to know, the other begged for answers.

'Why didn't you make a statement before now?' The sergeant reached for the notebook in his pocket.

Tameka looked him in the eye and squared her shoulders, releasing her grip on Harley's fingers. He placed a comforting hand on her back. She'd been through so much. He wanted to tell her to stop, to not say anything that would cause her more pain. But what the hell did she know about Ryan?

'Have you ever been so afraid of the truth that if you speak it, you'll only make things worse, Sergeant? That if you tell, someone else might get hurt?'

'I'm finding myself afraid of many things lately,' he confessed. 'Why now?'

'Because I have nothing left to lose. No-one to protect. And now I remember what I hadn't wanted to remember as a little girl.' Tameka turned to Shirley. 'My only regret is the pain this will cause the Bakers. I'm so sorry, Shirley, but as much as I need to see justice done for my mother, I need to see the same for Ryan. I only wish I'd known this for sure a long time ago, but it was only during the fire in the kitchen that day that the memory resurfaced.'

Cold, numb, and empty, Tameka tightened her fingers on the back of the chair. She'd agonised over telling the Bakers about what she thought she saw, a memory she was now convinced was the truth.

Her father's face that day, angry beyond reasoning, his temper out of control as he'd come back to the house smashing everything in his way. They'd hidden, her and Mum, until the firefighters had arrived, and Dad's temper had settled into a cold, empty, emotionless mask when they'd discovered Ryan's body inside the shed.

'The fire in the kitchen wasn't deliberate, but what started it escalated quickly. My father's — stepfather's — moods and temper have been out of control lately, more so than ever before. It didn't take much to set him off.'

Numb on the inside, she drew a breath then told them about the events leading up to dinner. How he'd come into the kitchen demanding his food, reacted angrily when it wasn't ready. Pushing her, cornering her against the range, ignoring the flames that licked at her shirt, kicking her, and stepping over her to leave her to burn.

Shirley pressed a hand to her mouth, uttered a cry and leaned against Tom. Harley's arm moved around Tameka's shoulders. She didn't want his sympathy. She didn't deserve it. Shrugging him away, she stepped over to the kitchen sink and looked out the window over the field of damaged hop bines Harley had started clearing, rubbing the scar on her temple.

'While I lay there watching the flames, I remembered the day Ryan died. I wasn't sure if it was a true memory or the exaggeration of an eight-year-old mind.'

Sergeant Riggs rocked on his feet. 'It's not unusual to suppress memories following a trauma. Especially in children.'

Tameka looked at her hands. 'After today … I'm still not sure, but I have to tell someone. Because if my father is capable of murdering my mother and leaving me to die in a fire, he's capable of what I thought I saw that day.'

Loki leaned against her leg and whimpered. She reached down to rub his ears, turned from the window, and sank to the floor next to him. She wrapped her arms around him and pressed her forehead to his warmth. Sensing her distress, Loki let her hold him, standing dead still.

'We'd come back up from the dam. Harley had gone

to look for his dad. I wanted to check on Ryan. He'd told us he was going to the shed to play inside the old ute he loved so much. I was afraid my dad would catch him in there and be angry with him. Dad liked his whip a little too much sometimes.'

'Tameka, you don't have to do this.' Harley crouched down in front of her. 'It might not be real.'

'It's real. I know it now.' She raised her eyes to his, held onto his gaze as the rest of the horrible truth poured out. He'd hate her. God, she hated herself for hurting him and his family all over again. 'When I got to the trees around the shed, I saw the flames. Then I saw Dad coming out of the shed. I wanted to shout, to warn him there was a fire, to check if Ryan was inside. I heard Ryan screaming, Dad laughing as he put the lock on the shed door.' Her breath hitched and tears stung her eyes as she remembered the two cruel sounds colliding. 'My father deliberately locked Ryan in the shed and left him to die. And I ran away.'

Shocked silence rocked the room. Harley stood and backed away, horror chasing disbelief from his face and replacing it with scorn. Had she expected anything less? She'd witnessed his brother's murder and said nothing. For almost twenty years. The man she'd loved in every which way possible would slip away from her again.

Tameka couldn't bear to look at the Bakers. The people who, even after Ryan's death, had still welcomed her into their home. And Sergeant Riggs, who'd seen far too many deaths than a town the size of Wongan Creek needed in its history.

Tameka kissed Loki's head, a final goodbye to the dog who trusted her explicitly, something she'd never know from humans again. She stood. 'I'll go down to the station with you now, Sergeant Riggs, and answer any questions the detectives have.'

She wanted to say sorry, to apologise for her father's sins, but the words wouldn't push past the lump of guilt in her throat. She wouldn't be coming back. The only way clear for her now was out of Wongan Creek.

Chapter Twenty-Three

Two weeks. Two of the longest bloody weeks of Harley's life during which Tameka's confessions had left his family reeling and bleeding from wounds they thought they'd had a bandage on even if they weren't healed completely.

Dad had to be admitted to hospital with chest pains as he'd relived the day of Ry's death over in his mind again. He'd been taken to Perth to see the heart surgeon, and the wait for news had been a long one.

Mum had withdrawn to deal with the revelations, the loss renewed, raw and bleeding because that disastrous day had never been far from her mind and Ry's memory had stayed close to her heart.

And the guilt, pain and loss of Ryan's death had haunted his dreams every night. If only … If only he'd not been distracted that day. If only he'd tried harder to make Ryan stay with them. If only he'd known back then what a monster Louis Chalmers really was.

Old man Chalmers — the lying, murderous bastard — had pleaded not guilty via video link and was now on his way to Perth to face court. It brought no comfort because nothing would ever bring his brother back and the actions of a vile and disgusting man had taken away two of the people he loved. Three if he counted Mai who he remembered as a quiet, reserved yet kind lady whose tentative smile grew whenever he and Tameka were together.

Harley tossed the pen down on his desk and pressed his fingers to his tired eyes. Behind him, the news on the telly reported that new DNA evidence had surfaced, and Louis Chalmers had been linked to another cold case murder that happened almost thirty years ago. A woman and two young girls now suspected to be his wife and children. Where would it end?

Golden Acres had been seized as the proceeds of crime when they'd uncovered evidence that Chalmers had come by the property illegally, forging the sale and transfer when he'd come across the original owner, Hugh Fisher, in a nursing home, suffering from dementia.

Perhaps not so coincidentally, the same nursing home had been destroyed by fire not long after the sale had gone through, a matter now under investigation again. It seemed Louis Chalmers had quite a fascination for lighting fires.

Tameka was officially homeless. If she ever returned from Perth. He doubted she would, and that broke his already trashed heart. She'd left with Riggs the day her father was charged with murder and had made it clear she had no intention of seeing him again.

Don't follow me, Harley. It's time you changed your menu.

Her words haunted him. He wanted to go to her, tell her it didn't matter as long as she came home to Bakers Hill. She wasn't to blame for Ryan's death or anyone else's.

She needs time to work through it, Harley. Give her the space to get the help she needs, to process ... the same as we need to.

And here he was, taking his mother's advice when he really wanted to be where Tameka was. When he wanted to be the one to help her, to understand all the things he didn't, and to give her the love and stability he hadn't known she didn't have.

If anything had happened to her ... if she'd died under Louis Chalmers' roof ... he didn't want to contemplate what that meant. She hadn't. He had to hold onto that little gem or drive himself insane. But Ryan had died at the hands of a ruthless murderer, and he couldn't forgive that.

He thought about going into town, to the pub to

hang out with his mates. Drink a beer or two, watch reruns of the footy season finals. Get away from the sight of the burnt homestead on Golden Acres and the equal emptiness that echoed off the walls of the house on Bakers Hill.

None of this was Tameka's fault. When they got through this — the court hearing and a conviction — maybe she'd find her way back to him. He'd give her a little time and space, knowing she'd have Heather Bailey by her side looking after her welfare. And when all this was over, he'd go looking for her and bring her home, spend the rest of his life helping her find happiness and peace.

Loki lay pining outside the door of the spare room, offering up the occasional doggy groan of despair. He'd even lost interest in washing dishes.

Harley understood. He'd lost interest in eating despite the tempting smell of the freshly made casserole Annie Hamilton had delivered this morning and the home-baked bread her mother had sent to compliment it.

Maybe he could hang out at the hardware store with Mal and Ahn, find out how well they'd known Mai since Ahn had been the closest to her. Do some research and trace the whereabouts of Mai's family village in case Tameka wanted to find them.

He could visit Ryan and tell him that his killer was being brought to justice, maybe find peace in his own heart for letting Ryan go to the shed that day.

He'd wanted to go to Perth for the hearing, but the demands of the farm and the delay in his application for a hardship grant meant he had to stay and manage the fallout. Look to the future of Bakers Hill for his father's sake. Make a haven for Tameka to come home to, if she wanted to, when she was ready.

He picked up a pencil from the stubby holder on his desk and began to sketch the idea forming in his mind.

The hits just kept coming. Five counts of murder. Tameka sat in the courtroom and listened numbly as the arguments and evidence against Louis piled up. She couldn't call him her father. Not since he'd confessed that she wasn't his blood. Mai had already been pregnant when he'd abducted her from the streets of Ho Chi Minh City's red-light district.

She had no right to Golden Acres at all because it was stolen property. She was officially homeless. Out of luck, out of love and out of money. Not to mention out of her depth in this big city with its towering buildings and busy streets where she had no hope of finding employment because all she knew was how to get her hands dirty on the land.

Today was the day the judge would hand down Louis' sentence. Tameka thanked whatever god had allowed the case to hit top priority on the list in the normally sluggish justice system, a two-year wait for a trial not unheard of with a shortage in the ratio of judges to courtrooms.

His lawyer had advised him to change his plea to guilty and the jury had been dismissed. How could he not be guilty when he'd confessed to the whole mess under questioning, some of the evidence had turned the judge's face white with shock. Louis could face a maximum sentence of life imprisonment, and if the judge had mercy on the community, it would be without parole.

She didn't even have the money to give her mother a decent burial when the case was closed, and her remains were released from evidence.

And damn it, her heart was breaking because she'd have to leave Harley and Loki behind. What man would want to be saddled with a woman who'd witnessed the murder of his brother and said nothing?

He wouldn't want the physically and emotionally scarred illegitimate daughter of a Vietnamese prostitute as his wife. The town of Wongan Creek, with all its problems, wouldn't want her kind of mix in their gene pool. Lovely people like Heather Bailey wouldn't want to be her friend, and Mal and Ahn would never serve her in their shop again, even with Harry running interference.

She thought of Casey's artwork tucked into the pocket of her jacket in the spare room at Bakers Hill, the freedom those butterflies represented. She'd glimpsed that Utopia for a short while, embraced it with Harley one last time, but like the picture she'd left behind, she'd have to abandon her dreams for reality and live a new kind of hell in a different prison.

She'd have to pull up her ugly, brown-striped, donated panties, be a big girl and toughen up on the streets of Perth. Maybe someone in Northbridge would give her a break and a job waitressing.

The room she had at the YWCA would have to do for a while longer, but they'd already said it was only temporary if she couldn't pay the long-term resident's fee.

Behind her, the door to the courtroom opened and closed. Another reporter, another curious citizen. But it wasn't a reporter who slipped into the seat beside her.

Shirley Baker's warm hand covered her cold one. 'Hello, sweetheart. Tom had to see the heart surgeon. We wanted to check up on you and see how you're coping,' she whispered.

Tameka blinked back the unexpected sting of tears. She couldn't allow herself to crumble when she had to be strong to stand alone. 'I'm fine, thank you.'

The judge adjourned to make his decision on the sentence to be handed down and the courtroom cleared as Louis was taken from the dock.

'Come downstairs and have a coffee with us. We'll stay with you for the sentencing.'

'That's really not necessary, Shirley, but thank you.'

Tom touched her shoulder. 'Not necessary, no. But we'd like to talk to you, love.'

Tameka didn't want to talk. Not about Louis, or Ryan or Harley. That the Bakers were even here blew her away. Surprised her, because surely they'd never want to see the Chalmers family again. How could they not be angry, upset, and revengeful over the truth about the way their son had died?

They had to be. God knows, she was angry herself. Angry that she hadn't done more to stop Ryan from going up to the shed at all. Angry for not being old enough or strong enough to stop any of this madness from happening.

Shirley sighed, hooked an arm through hers and coaxed her towards the bank of elevators. 'You're probably thinking all this is your fault. Well, it's not.' She pressed the down arrow on the panel on the wall. 'You didn't put the padlock on that door, sweetheart.'

'No, but I might as well have.' Tameka looked at Shirley. Yes, Harley's mum was upset. The glimmer of tears and dark circles under her eyes said she hadn't had much sleep since their life imploded either.

'I'm so sorry. I wish …'

Shirley squeezed her arm as the elevator doors opened. 'We all wish we could turn back the clock and change things, bring Ryan back, but we can't. A conviction, a sentence, nothing can undo the harm that's been done. We want to remember Ryan and Mai the way they were before. It happened and now the man responsible will pay his penance. Justice is served for Ryan. And for Mai. It's enough. And Louis will stand trial again for Ryan's murder and the others. I'm angry, yes, but not at you. My regret, sweetheart, is that you've had to suffer through what you have alone.'

They stepped inside the elevator and the doors swished closed. Tameka leaned her head back against the cool, steel-sheeted walls, the tension headache that had seized her on the day of Louis' arrest and not let go pounding behind her eyes.

No, nothing would bring Ryan back, and the nightmare would fade, but the fallout would reverberate through Wongan Creek for years to come.

She could never return and find happiness with Harley. Not after all this. He was better off finding someone else. A girl like Annie who was worthy of the respect of the town.

'It's not even a comfort knowing he's not my real father.' Her words echoed around the steel car. 'He's the only father I've known.'

And her mother would still be alive if she'd never met him that night in Ho Chi Minh City. Ryan and those poor girls in Cook's Harbour would still be alive. And she'd never have met Harley, the man who owned her heart, body, and soul.

'Harley misses you, sweetheart. He wanted to come

but this business with the bank and the National Farmers' Federation has him tied to the farm. Please come home when this is over?'

'I can't, Shirley. I don't belong in Wongan Creek or on Bakers Hill. I don't know where I belong.'

'You belong with us, Tameka. There'll always be a place at our table for you. We don't hold a grudge against you for what Louis did. He hurt you as much as he hurt us. Your mum would want us to take care of you. I wish you could have come to us for help sooner so it didn't have to come to this.' Shirley took Tameka's hand in hers.

Wouldn't that be nice? To belong to a real family again. To come home to warm and loving arms after a long day out in the fields. To be a part of a nurturing environment, something neither she nor her mum had ever had. But that was a pipedream when her every step in life had been shaped by a murderer. When she would always be known as Louis Chalmers' daughter, even when she wasn't his blood.

'Do you remember, sweetheart, how after Ryan died you and Harley were inseparable? The two of you always had such a strong bond, but it grew even stronger. Don't throw that kind of love away because you think you don't deserve it.' Shirley patted Tameka's hand and squeezed her fingers. 'If it wasn't for you, he would have struggled even more to get over Ryan's death. Let him help you over this hurdle. You two belong together. We've always known that.'

'I need time to work it all out.' Time and distance to process thoughts that would drive her to the edge of reason trying to understand. To dig out of the hole she'd been buried in forever, and to take that step towards freedom when she'd been a prisoner to guilt for so long.

'Then take all the time you need. The door will still be open at Bakers Hill. Wongan Creek will still be there. There's talk in town of new ventures, better prospects other than the gold mine. It seems like exactly the right time to be building new relationships or rekindling old ones.'

The doors swished open, and they stepped out of the elevator towards the coffee shop.

Tom put his arm around Tameka's shoulders. 'You'll always be family to us, Tameka. I mean, how could you not be, for God's sake? My wife bought you sexy underwear to model for our son, that's practically a marriage proposal.'

Tameka couldn't stop the laugh that built in her throat as she hugged Tom hard. Maybe she did have a real dad after all, but first she needed to deal with a killer and lay a ghost to rest.

Three days later the gates clanged shut behind Tameka on the visitor's cell at Casuarina's maximum security prison facility.

At the square table bolted to the floor, Louis

Chalmers sat handcuffed, dressed in orange prison overalls that leeched the colour from his skin.

She didn't see her father. She saw a murderous monster wearing the battle scars of a drinking problem and a mental health issue. The prison psychologists would have a field day mapping out his mind. What drove a man to murder other than insanity?

He didn't speak, only stared at her as if she were a stranger rather than the person who'd cooked his meals, washed his laundry, farmed land that wasn't his and felt the full force of his wrath.

'Why?' She didn't sit in the chair opposite the thick glass barrier that separated them. She didn't want to come down to his level where he could control her ever again.

He leaned back in the chair, no longer the big, scary man he'd been, diminished by the legal system and at the mercy of inmates who had no patience for child killers.

He didn't pretend not to know what she was asking. 'She was useless to me. She told me you were a boy. I needed a boy.' He leaned forward, his eyes dark and mean. 'She gave me a girl. Always girls. The other one was the same.'

'So, you killed them? All of them.'

'Yes. It's what you do when a mare doesn't breed. You slaughter it.'

Tameka swallowed the bitter taste on her tongue. He

wasn't human. But deep down, she'd always known that. Yet she'd stayed on the farm to protect him, to stop him shooting himself. Only now she knew it wasn't suicide he'd been planning.

'And Ryan?'

'Little shit was sniffing around where he didn't need to be. Didn't seem fair that Baker had a healthy wife and two sons, and I had nothing. If the other boy had taken the lure, they'd both be dead.'

Tameka shivered. How close had Harley been to death too? 'What did it matter that I wasn't a boy? I worked like one.'

'You really are a stupid girl, aren't you? I should have finished the job properly instead of leaving you to burn. Fed you to Baker's pigs instead.'

She tried not to let it hurt, tried not to feel disgusted by his lack of regret for his actions. This was on him, not her. This insane hang up with fathering a son and failing at it didn't make sense. Perhaps he really was insane, and reason didn't factor in his head at all.

'A man isn't a man until he's sired a son. My stepfather beat that into me any which way he could and then he left me with the lying, cheating bitch who gave birth to me. So, I killed her and then I went looking for him. He'd found another vessel to produce a son he could be proud of.' He leaned forward and gripped his cuffed hands together on the table, self-satisfaction glowing in his eyes. 'I watched the house burn. You have no idea the power fire gives a man. To kill, destroy. To eliminate the cause of your pain.'

Jesus, he really was crazy. A pyromaniac serial killer she'd shared a home with for twenty-seven years. A man with an agenda and a twisted mind. That she'd survived at all was a miracle. That he'd waited so long after Ryan and her mother's death to strike again incomprehensible.

The tiny, clinical room closed in on her as she turned away from the man she'd once called her father. She had the answers she'd come for and now the urge escalated to leave, to escape the poisoned mind in the room. With one last look at the monster who'd taken her life hostage and whom she wouldn't let control her anymore, she left to arrange her mother's burial. No cremation. There'd been enough destruction by fire.

Chapter Twenty-Four

He'd seen her walk up from the dam, across the field of wilted and forgotten barley on the land the Chalmers no longer owned. Had never lawfully owned. He'd tried to keep his heart in his chest, but he suspected it was beating away on his sleeve for everyone to see, as it had been since she left.

'Still perfecting the rinse cycle?' Tameka hitched her backpack higher on her shoulder as she approached and watched Loki lick Harley's plate clean.

She'd lost weight she couldn't afford to lose, and her features were pale and drawn. It broke his heart to see her this way. If she stayed, he'd fix that. 'Loki's a pro at dishes now. One day soon he'll be standing at the sink with dish liquid and a sponge in his paws.'

Loki barked his agreement before bolting over to Tameka and nudging her hand for an ear scratch.

'He's calmed down a lot.'

Harley grimaced. 'We've had a lot of time on our hands to practice obedience and manners. How'd things go in Perth?'

He'd heard it on the news. Louis Chalmers had changed his plea to guilty and been detained without bail on five counts of murder. The judge had delivered a sentence of life imprisonment without parole, sparing no mercy, and making it almost impossible to appeal.

'It's over. That's all that counts.'

'So, what now?'

Tameka shrugged. 'I've come to say goodbye, I guess.'

'Such an overrated word. The National Farmers Federation has overturned the application for compensation given that the issue of spray drift is no longer a danger to the crops. All proposed action has been withdrawn. You're free of blame, Tikki. Do you really want to leave?' He didn't want her to go. There was finally some hope of a future for everyone in Wongan Creek. If she didn't want a future with him, maybe she'd stick around town so he could make sure she was safe. 'Ninety percent of us have had our hardship grants approved to allow our crops time to recover. The other ten percent have sold out to John Bannister. Mostly those with property bordering the mine to allow for expansion.'

'I'm not sure I can stay, Harley. Too many ghosts.

Too many questions and fingers to be pointed. A change of town, new people … maybe it will be different. I have to try. But I couldn't leave without explaining it all to you first.'

Harley rubbed a hand over Loki's head. 'Leave? I didn't figure you for a coward, Tikki.'

'You didn't figure me being the daughter of a killer either.'

'But you're not, are you?'

'No, but I am the daughter of a prostitute and I'll never know who my real father is.' She toed the ground with her boot.

'I fell in love with a girl like that once. Still love her. I wonder where she is now. She was such a brave girl. Mouthy, stubborn, built tough.' Harley stood and walked down the veranda steps, his hands itching to touch her. He pushed them into the pockets of his jeans. 'Her name was Tikki, and she was my best friend.'

'She's gone, Harley. Maybe she never existed. Maybe she was always a fake.'

'I disagree. There was nothing fake about what we had between us.' Harley stood close and placed his hand next to hers until they touched on Loki's collar. 'Why didn't you come to me for help?'

'I couldn't.'

'Why not?'

Tameka shivered. 'Because I was afraid.'

'Of what?'

'Of having to admit that big, strong, independent Tameka Chalmers could fix a bloody ute, manhandle a seeder box and sow a God damn field of barley single-handedly, but she was afraid to leave a father who didn't deserve the title.'

'Why didn't you leave?' He wished he understood what had kept her there, what had made her subject herself to the denigration and humiliation day after day when she could have walked away through the gate onto Bakers Hill at any time.

'And right there is the question I'm so afraid of people asking, Harley. The one everyone asks regardless, but never really understands the answer to. "Why didn't you just walk away, Tameka?" Like it's so easy to turn around and say, "Hey, I'm not taking your crap anymore, old man" and walk out the door as if there'd be no consequences, no fallout, no harm or foul and no-one would get hurt. If only it were that easy.'

She turned away from him to face the rolling fields of Golden Acres where all her hard work had turned brown and wilted. Harley wanted to reach for her, hold her while she told her story, but he knew if he did she'd shut down on him and those secrets would fester inside her forever.

He'd done his research, read the reasons victims stayed in abusive relationships or felt a misguided loyalty to abusive parents. He understood that until Tameka could voice her fears and talk about the last eight years, she'd never begin to heal. So, he stood in silence and let her talk, even though it was Loki she told her story to, not him.

'I floundered between feeling helpless to stand up against him, wanting to leave, wanting to stay, and wishing he was dead. Wishing that he would take his gun and shoot himself because that was the only way I'd ever be free of him. I made excuses for his behaviour. Poor Dad — heartbroken that his wife left him with a useless daughter to run the farm. I tried harder to please him, to make him proud of me for something … anything. And now I find out he knew I wasn't even his daughter. He'd put up with me all this time. For nothing. No wonder he treated me the way he did.'

She sighed, a shaky sound that ate at his heart until it ached, but he couldn't help until she was done with her story, until all the hurt and blame had been purged from her system. He wanted to tell her she didn't deserve to be emotionally or physically abused — no-one did — but she wouldn't believe him until she believed it herself.

'No wonder he took his temper out on me. I continually felt as if I was to blame for the situation he was in and if I left, I'd be responsible for his downfall. That Golden Acres would be lost completely. I loved the land too much to let that happen, never considering for a moment that it might never be mine. If I left Louis, I'd leave behind the memories, the only piece of Mum I had. I'd leave Ryan who didn't deserve to die. And you, Harley. I'd leave behind my heart, my reason to keep breathing even if you weren't mine to have.'

She sank to her knees with her arms around Loki, who settled into her cuddle and rested his head against hers, his ice-blue eyes sad as he looked at Harley over her shoulder.

'I'll never be able to make people understand that while I had the choice to leave, I couldn't, even though I knew I should. That I could never tell anyone what I'd seen him do to Ryan in case he did it to me too. Selfish of me, isn't it?' She gave a self-deprecating laugh. 'And then he left me to die in that fire, the same way he did Ryan. Yet still I protected him. What kind of a weak fool am I?'

Harley folded his arms across his chest to stop them from reaching for her. 'That's one thing you're not, Tikki. You're nobody's fool.'

'People will never understand that though. Not unless they're victims themselves. Some days I don't even understand why I stayed. I'm a fool for staying, a fool for letting him treat me the way he did, a fool for not leaving. Look what happened to Mum when she walked away.' Tameka shook her head. 'I'm a fool for that too. For believing she left me with him, that she'd deserted me, and I wasn't worth taking along. So, I stayed with the parent who did want me until I learnt he didn't want me at all. How messed up is that?'

'You could have come to us. Mum would have taken you in a heartbeat.' He wished she had so he could have spared her the horror of what she'd been through.

'How could I? You were away in Perth studying, your dad wasn't well even back then, and your mum had her hands full helping him run the farm. She didn't need my dramas added to hers. Besides, they were no match for Louis' temper. Imagine what he would have done to your parents if I'd left to stay with them? He killed his own wife, chopped her up and buried her in a suitcase at the bottom of a dam. He let an innocent young boy burn to death for no other reason than Ryan was playing in his shed.'

'Ryan's death wasn't your fault, Tikki. No-one thinks it was.'

'That's not true, Harley. You did. You believed it. That day in the kitchen when I told Riggs what happened. I saw your face. For a moment there, you blamed me.'

'I was in shock. You were eight at the time. It's not as if you locked that damn door yourself. There was nothing you could do to change what happened that day. Nothing I could do either.' He had to make her understand that they were powerless to stop the events that took place that day, no matter how much it hurt knowing Ryan's death wasn't an accident. 'No matter how much I wish life could have been different for all of us.'

'You know what the worst thing is, Harley?' She released her hold on Loki and stood to face him. 'Every day I held onto the hope that things would change. He was the man I was meant to love like a father and couldn't, the man I looked to for protection, a job, and a roof over my head. I tried to change my approach. I thought if I did what he wanted, I'd make him happy, make up for my mother leaving, for the wreck the farm had become as he deliberately destroyed it bit by bit.' She laughed, the sound raw and bitter. 'All I succeeded in doing was to give myself false hope I couldn't let go of.'

'But you're free now to start a new life, build new hope for the future. Let me help you be the person you want to be. I love you, Tikki. I always have. And I should have had the balls to take you away from him before now, except I wasn't sure you'd come.'

'I wouldn't have come. I couldn't. Not as long as I was tied to my father … my *step*father … by violence, guilt, and failure. Heather helped me understand that. I've never stopped loving you, Harley, but I'm not who I used to be.'

Finally, she admitted to still loving him. Hope glowed in his heart. 'Then let me help you be somebody you want to be. Who are you, Tikki?'

'I am Tameka Nguyen.' She whispered it as if testing the name with the universe to see if it brought her better luck.

'There you go. A new name, a new start. Let it be with me.'

'I'll always be nobody.'

'And do you really think that matters out here when we're struggling to grow whatever we can and keep a town in balance? To stop it from being consumed by a hole in the ground that will be abandoned when the vein of gold runs out. When with every fire we put out, another one flares up?'

The mention of fire made her wince, and he regretted using the analogy. By now even the worst of her burns would almost be healed over, but the pain would stay with her forever and even when it faded, the scars would still be there to remind her. Like the hole in his heart left by the truth of Ryan's death, even though his own guilt still ate at him.

He should have told Dad that day that Ryan had gone into Louis' shed, but instead, he'd become distracted by driving the tractor for the first time with Dad's guidance and all thought of Ryan had been lost until it was too late. They were kids and it was no-one's fault but Louis Chalmers' who'd chosen to take a life that day.

Harley reached out to touch Tameka's face, his palm cupping her cheek. 'You're my nobody and I love you for who you are. Stay, Tikki. Stay and help me rebuild Bakers Hill. Be my wife, my partner, my ally. Be a mum to Loki and if you like it, we'll have more — human or canine, whatever you want.' He tipped up her chin. 'Be Tameka Nguyen-Baker, and I'll even wash the dishes after Loki's put them through the rinse cycle and not put them straight back in the cupboard.'

'You never did that anyway, you tool.'

He felt her lips stretch in a smile under his, so he kissed her until her hands fisted into his shirt and her hips moulded against him then he kissed her some more.

'You know how to tempt a girl,' she whispered when he let her come up for air.

'Come inside and I'll show you my full line-up. If you're not convinced by the end of it, I'll drive you wherever you want to go, even if it's Far North Queensland.'

'The opposite end of the country? That's a long way to drive to get rid of me, Harley. Can you be away from Bakers Hill for that long?' she teased before her brow creased in a frown and she caught her lip between her teeth. 'I don't know ...'

He released his hold on her hips and took her hand instead. 'Come with me. We'll stop by my office where I'll show you the plans to turn Bakers Hill into the Bed and Breakfast Mum always wanted, a hilltop adventure trail called Ryan's Ridge and a dam called Mai's Pond.' Harley tugged her up the veranda stairs.

'What about the research grant application?'

Harley grinned. He was fairly sure she'd like his

plan. 'All going ahead. You know how Golden Acres was seized as the proceeds of crime?'

She nodded.

'Well, property and any funds seized are deposited into a Confiscated Assets Account managed by the Australian Financial Security Authority. Since Wongan Creek is a town currently experiencing hardship on the agricultural front, I've submitted an application for the land to be used to benefit the community through a crop research and development scheme. The crop research facility will provide jobs for those who want to stay in farming rather than join the exodus to work for Wongan Creek Mining. The community is keen to work to bring stability to the area again in both industries. The proposal is on the Attorney-General's desk as we speak, and John Bannister has committed funds towards the scheme too.'

'Wow, that's big news, Baker.'

'Yep, and because of the fire damage I've also made an application for funds to restore the homestead and list it as a heritage building as it was intended.' He tugged her into his study over to his desk covered with roughly drawn plans.

Tameka dragged her hand from his and picked up the one showing Mai's Pond with a peaceful arbour next to the dam for shade and a swing surrounded by a Vietnamese-inspired garden. She put it down and picked up Ryan's Ridge with its adventure trail that included an old ute exactly like the one Ryan had discovered in Louis' shed. Her hands shook on the paper.

'Still want to leave, Tikki?' He bloody hoped not. Harley leaned his butt against the desk and drew the plans out of her hands. 'Say you'll stay and build this dream with me.'

'I had a dream once.'

He tugged her into the V of his legs and held her steady by her hips. 'Tell me.'

'I wanted to open a cooking school at the homestead, grow organic veggies and create exotic dishes with my students.'

'Then stay, and we'll build your dream too. I don't see the Heritage Council having a problem with that. It will go well with the proposed brewery facility and provide a lunch and dinner menu for the Bed and Breakfast guests.'

She lifted her hands to his face, and he pressed his cheek against her palm. 'I'm sorry, Harley. For everything. I want to believe in love, acceptance, and dreams that come true, but every time I open my eyes or turn around, I see only disappointment and destruction.'

'Then let me change your view of the world. Things are changing for the better in Wongan Creek. Sure, we'll have more trials and disasters, but we've proved we have successes too.'

'They'll never accept me. Not after what my father … what Louis did.'

'I think you'll be surprised. No-one blames you. They'll have questions, yes, but everyone in this town is battling to keep their own skeletons buried. No-one will be pointing fingers at anyone.' He held her gaze, strong and steady, read the insecurity and doubt in her eyes. 'You have people in your corner fighting with you not against you.'

'Three people against a whole town? I'm not sure of the odds on that one.'

'Never underestimate the power of a woman named Shirley Baker.' He grinned. 'Mum's already paving the way for you in town. You've been invited to join the CWA. They're planning an afternoon tea welcome as soon as you're settled in.'

'You're that sure I'll stay?'

'Yes.'

'You're a cocky bastard. What if I say no?'

He trailed a finger down her throat, slipped it under the collar of her shirt and located the zipper on her onesie. He gave it a little flick. He was pretty keen to see how her burns had healed and to remove as many of the scars life had left on her as he could.

'I'll have to find another way to convince you.' He gathered her in his arms, picked her up and held her close to his heart. Loki gave a little whine of approval and fell into step at his side.

'I might take a lot of convincing,' she whispered

against his throat as he carried her down the hallway to his bedroom. 'And a lot of healing too.'

He grinned as he let her slide down his body, his hands steadying her as she went. 'I was hoping you would, and I believe I'm the right man for the job. I'm happy to show you my credentials.'

'I've seen your credentials.' She lifted her mouth to his and whispered against his lips, 'Now show me the reason to stay.'

'I'll never hurt you, Tikki. That's a promise from the depth of my heart, and my heart is yours, so I'll tread very carefully. Please don't go.'

'I love you, Harley Baker.'

His smile grew wider, and his heart beat harder. He had the chance to make her happy again. He had the rest of his life to make sure she knew how much he loved her right back. Starting now.

'Sorry, Loki, private party,' he said as he pushed the door closed with his foot.

THE END

Shadows (Wongan Creek Series Book 3)

Want to know what happens next in Wongan Creek? Join Fenella and Kieran on their journey to find justice at The Cranky Lizard Winery.

Shadows (Wongan Creek Series Book 3)
   by Juanita Kees

When the shadows ride in Wongan Creek...

Fenella Rose-Waterman is happy running The Cranky Lizard winery until a broken relationship lifts the lid on the Pandora's Box of her past. After years of repressed memories haunting her dreams, she is forced to face the truth to find justice. But with truth comes a danger that puts everyone she loves at risk.

Kieran Murphy left Wongan Creek a newlywed and returned a widower. He believes he and his young son will find healing in the town that healed him once before. Instead, he finds the woman he loved running scared, her life in turmoil and her business under threat.

As the shadows of the past gather on the horizon, will they lose their chance of happiness, or will they find healing together?

Chapter One

Fen drew in a deep breath and let it out on a sigh as she lined up shot glasses on the scarred wooden bar at The Cranky Lizard winery. 'How could I have been so stupid, Sarge?'

'There's nothing stupid about you, Fenella. You were simply an easy mark.' Sergeant Riggs closed his notepad and tucked it into his uniform pocket. 'It's not a reflection on your intelligence. It's more a sign of how smart organised crime is becoming and how easy it is for these guys to target people like you and Liv.'

'You'd think I'd have recognised the tactics though.' Luke Sampson had charmed his way into her heart and home, then he'd wormed his way into the winery accounts and stolen Murray and Liv's lifetime of hard work. All because she'd believed the lies of a thief.

'Men like Sampson see the scars, the wristbands, the

piercings and the dark clothing, and they see a rebel, someone who has a score to settle with the world. They don't see where you've come from or where you've been. They don't know who you've grown into or what you've become. They only see the wounds from a past that can be reopened and made to fester.'

And no matter how hard she tried to ignore her past, it kept coming back to slap her on the arse. The rebellious child nobody had wanted because she self-harmed. The inexplicable, deep-seated fear that haunted the shadows at night, the ingrained terror of a memory that refused to surface. And the confusion of being shunted from one foster family to another, not knowing how long she'd be there before her actions would have her carers rethinking their decision.

No-one had understood the devil that drove her until the Watermans had taken her in and helped her turn her life around. Liv had been more of a mum to her than Antoinette had ever been.

Fen shook off the thought of Antoinette the way she always did, the same way she pushed aside the nightmares that caught her unaware in the middle of the night. 'So, what happens now?'

'There'll be an investigation. Fraud squad will take over and turn your life upside down. They'll go through the winery's books with a fine-tooth comb. Every transaction, every movement will be scrutinised. You'll be questioned and cross-questioned until they can eliminate you as an accomplice, given your intimate relationship with Sampson.'

She pulled a face. 'If only I hadn't given in to his nagging for a date. But he wouldn't give up until I said yes.' It had seemed like the perfect way to take a step forward, out of her comfort zone, away from the hope that, one day, Kieran Murphy might come home. 'Showing up here every day in his lunch break, on weekends. Making me believe how much he hated his job at the mine.'

Riggs chuckled. 'Unfortunately, there are good people and bad people in this world, young lady, and sometimes it's hard to tell them apart. Sometimes they pretend to care, yet all the time they're carrying a knife in their lunchbox, waiting for the opportunity to stab you in the back with it. You were unlucky to get one of those. Not that I'm surprised he picked you. You've grown into a fine young lass. A man would have to have rocks in his head not to notice that. If you were my daughter, I'd have the shotgun loaded twenty-four-seven.'

Fen leaned across the bar and patted his arms. 'Cheers for that.'

Riggs' smile faded back into his usual mask of seriousness. 'Be careful, Fen. The men Sampson answers to don't play games. There's a reason they infiltrate small towns. It's much easier to hide things out here.'

Fen shivered. 'I found that out the hard way, Sarge.'

Her jaw still ached where Luke's knuckles had made contact the day she'd found his cuts hidden in a box under their bed and dared to ask about them. That had been her final clue that Luke Sampson wasn't the guy who liked red wine and sunsets and walks on the beach or hitting the surf with his board on a Sunday morning. And his Harley wasn't for recreation only.

All the other clues had been there in plain sight, except she'd been too blind to see them. And by the time she'd had the blinkers ripped off, it was too late. He'd taken off with a million dollars of their bank balance and left her with a hectare of growth down the back paddock — that *wasn't* grapevines — to explain to police.

'He'll pay for that too, Fen. I promise you that.' Riggs straightened and slapped a hand on the bar. 'I've got to get back into town. Say hi to Liv for me, okay?'

A rowdy group entered the cellar, led by their tour group operator. Her travelling bachelor party had arrived. 'Will do, Sarge.'

He paused and looked across to where Liv stood in deep conversation with a man Fen had been trying not to look at since he'd stepped through the door. 'You'd be happy Murphy's back in town?'

Her heart did that little skip-dance it always did whenever she thought of Kieran. 'I'm happy he answered the ad for a new manager. He has the skills and experience. Turning the winery around and fixing the mess I've made is all that matters now.' There, she'd put him in the safety zone where he couldn't rock her world again. Not when it had already been rocked because she'd taken a wrong turn trying to get over him.

Riggs studied her intently for a minute before making way for the tour group. 'Don't keep your blinkers on forever, okay? Wounds heal, and we forget our mistakes. Eventually. Take care, Fen. I'll be in touch.' He turned to the group. 'You boys stay out of trouble now. I don't want to have to come back here today.'

As she poured the first round for the group, Fen realised Liv was right about one thing — getting back to business was a whole lot better for her than crying into a coffee mug over a no-good, lying thief who didn't deserve her tears. Her relationship with Luke Sampson had only proved what she'd already suspected. Men were trouble.

Not all men are bastards, Fen love. You need to believe that, or you'll never find happiness.

Liv's words echoed through her thoughts. Confident words from a woman who'd been married to her soulmate, a gentle giant and true hero, whose sudden passing from a heart attack had left a huge gap in their lives. He'd gone into town for supplies and he hadn't come back. There one day, gone the next.

She let her gaze stray towards Liv, deep in

conversation with the man who had once been her rock and confidante. Kieran Murphy. Her heart hovered between stop and go. She'd loved him with every essence of her being. Until he'd tilted her world on an axis that had only just found balance and married Diane.

She steadied her hand as she poured a liqueur and concentrated on not spilling any. She shouldn't be this happy to see him when she'd lost him all those years ago, and the bond between them had been broken by distance and jealousy.

From across the room, those see-all eyes met hers with a flash of pleasure that took her breath away. Kieran had always had that power. A wave of memories played through her mind. There'd been a time when he'd brought happiness and light to her world of darkness. Until distance had silenced it all. The smile. The love. The friendship. Everything.

Strong fingers clamped around her leather wristband, the rough edges of the rawhide scraping against her scars, startling her out of her musings.

'I *said*, could I have a tasting round, please.'

Something in the man's tone — an inflection, a bite — had her stiffening as his hold tightened. Her gaze shot to his, caught sight of the tattoo under his left eye. The same teardrop design Luke wore on his left bicep, the only difference being this man's one had been coloured in whereas Luke's had been clear.

She shivered against the unease that knotted her belly and tried to keep her voice steady. 'If you let go of my hand, I'll pour you a drink. The prices are on the wine list.'

'A nice girl like you should pay more attention to her surroundings. Someone could get hurt while you're not looking.' He delivered the words through lips pulled tight over yellowed teeth, his soulless grey eyes set in a round face, tanned by the sun and weathered by the wind.

Memories swirled through her mind. A past that should stay forgotten in a place with dark hallways and shadowy corners. Men with secrets to keep, and Antoinette, the woman who serviced them. Men just like this one from a dark and dirty underworld where crime paid for sex and drugs. A life no child should be exposed to. Nausea burned in her throat, perspiration dampened the collar of her shirt and terror crept in from the shadows of her mind as the scars under her wristbands itched.

Kieran's warmth and solid strength filled the space behind her. 'Do we have a problem here?'

The man removed his fingers from her wrist. 'Your bartender here is a little slow. I was just trying to catch her attention.' He straightened, the faded patches on his worn leather vest coming into view. 'But it's okay. I'm not thirsty anymore.' He slapped ten dollars onto the bar, the rings on his tattooed knuckles catching the sunlight. 'That should cover it.' His eyes found Fen's. 'Take care now.'

Kieran crossed his arms and watched as the man made his way out the door. 'Want to tell me what that was all about?'

Fen waited until the flyscreen door closed before she turned to face him, praying he wouldn't see the terror she could almost taste. 'Unhappy customer. I had it under control.' She took slow breaths to control the hammering of her heart against her ribs and the fear that twisted her belly into knots. She was being watched by Luke's club members. The reality of that sank into her mind like a stone thrown into the koi pond out the front.

'Don't lie to me, Fen. I may have been away a while, but I still recognise trouble when I see it.'

Her heart did a backward somersault as he bent to kiss her cheek, greeting her the way he always had. Before he went away. She ignored the impulse to kiss him back, the way she would have done years ago. His long silence had hurt, their friendship the sacrifice he'd made in the name of commitment. Still, she couldn't deny the flicker of happiness that chased some of the fear from her mind. Kieran Murphy had come home, and she'd always felt safe when he was near.

'Welcome back.'

'Thank you.' The smile he offered her no longer reached his eyes or lit up his face the way it used to.

Dark shadows and a drawn look hinted at stress and sleepless nights.

Liv stepped up to the bar and sent her a look that told Fen she'd recognised the patches and the threat. 'Are you okay, love?'

'I'm okay, Mum. He's gone now.' She squeezed her mum's hand reassuringly.

Liv had enough to worry about, but it would be hard to ignore the warning in the man's presence so soon after they'd filed charges on Luke. Fen closed her thoughts to the fear that tried to sneak in again. She had to trust that Riggs would keep them safe. She wouldn't let herself be controlled by fear again. Fen turned to Kieran.

'How long do you need to think about taking the job?' One thing she could be certain of was that Kieran would know how to fix what Luke had broken. Everything except her heart.

'I can't make snap decisions here, Fen. It's not just me I have to think about.' A hint of sadness flickered in his expression and that trademark smile tugged down at the corners.

Of course, he'd have a family to consider. The tiny two-bedroomed cottage at the end of Blue Lizard Lane might not be big enough if he had children.

A lick of pain tightened her chest. Children. She rubbed at her wrists. There'd been a time once when she'd wanted to have kids, but every time she felt the itch of the scars, she was reminded of the past and all the reasons she shouldn't. A past haunted by memories that flickered out of reach on the peripheral of her mind. Monsters that lay buried until something triggered them and they rose to taunt her. Like the man at the bar.

'Fen, I'm going to take Kieran out to the cottage for a look. Would you mind keeping an eye on young Liam for us?'

'Liam?'

Kieran smiled. 'My son. He's four.' He looked at her through eyes that shone with pride and a warmth that, until now, had been missing.

A weight of regret settled in her stomach. Kieran would be a great dad. He'd overcome the monsters of his past, reached beyond the same barriers that kept her locked into their grip. The tour group leader signalled her for their bill. 'Give me a moment to take care of this, then I'm free for a while.' A distraction was exactly what she needed, and kids weren't nearly as complicated as adults or as threatening as cuts on a leather vest. 'Where is he?'

Liv waved a hand over to the play area. 'He's out there exploring. Take a bottle of apple juice out to him, would you, love?'

'Does he have a favourite topic he likes to talk about? To break the ice?'

A sad look crossed Kieran's features. 'He doesn't talk much these days.'

She wanted to ask why, but the grim pull to Kieran's lips had her swallowing on the question. There'd be time later for explanations. 'Okay, I'll see what I can find for him to do.'

Fen settled the tour group's bill, thanking them before she walked over to the fridge and pulled out a bottle of apple juice. If Kieran accepted the job, could she cope with watching them together every day? Her best friend, his wife and their perfect, happy family?

'Thanks.' Kieran squeezed her shoulder as he passed her to follow Liv out the door.

She watched him walk away, different yet the same, a set to his shoulders she hadn't seen since they were troubled teens arriving in Wongan Creek. With a sigh, she headed for the playground to find Liam. It stood eerily quiet and empty. Where were the sounds of a child playing? The tinkle of bells and spin of plastic blocks on metal poles, the delighted giggles of a ride down the slide.

Her breath caught in her throat as her thoughts slipped back to the man in the leather vest and the warning in his parting words. She shook them off. No, men like him didn't act on their threats immediately. And strangers wouldn't be their target. Men like him would strike at something much closer to home. Had Luke sent him to warn her to back off? As soon as things settled, she'd call Riggs with an update on the stranger's visit.

Fen pulled off the plastic seal around the top of the juice bottle and called out, 'Hey, Liam. My name is Fen. Your dad asked me to bring you an apple juice.'

Silence met her call and her heart took a little dip. Another quick look around showed all the gates surrounding the play area were closed.

'Liam?' She edged closer to the play equipment, searching the windows of a yellow cubby, the clear panel on the red tunnel that housed the interactive play boards, and the green platform with the periscope and pirate flag.

A little sniffle reached her ears from the tunnel that covered the slide. She leaned over to look inside. At the top of the slide, a little boy sat crouched over with his knees hugged to his chest and his head resting on a grubby-looking stuffed toy.

'Are you okay up there, mate?'

A mop of brown curls shivered as the little boy shook his head. A soft sob escaped his chest and he buried his face deeper into the stuffed toy.

'Okay, so your dad asked me to bring you a drink while he and my mum go and look at the cottage where you'll be staying.' Where was Diane? Why wasn't she here to take care of her son? 'Do you think you'd like to live here?'

Breath-stealing sobs echoed down the tunnel. Fen sat down on the edge of the slide. 'Why don't you come down and tell me what's making you sad? Maybe I can help.' The boy's heart-breaking sobs made her eyes sting with tears and her throat clog up. Fen patted the space next to her. 'If you come down, I'll make you a special drink. It's one of my favourites. Do you like lizards?'

At the top of the slide, Liam sucked in a breath and let it out on a word. 'Dunno.'

She'd kill for curls like his. Rich brown hair touched with caramel, just like his dad's. Did he have Diane's eyes?

'I like lizards. A lot. How about I make you a special drink called the Grumpy Lizard and you tell me if you like it or not? It comes with a lizard straw. The lizard's feet hook over the side of the cup. I'll let you keep it when you're done. Would you like that?'

Liam stretched out his legs, a teary look in his eyes the exact same shade as Kieran's. He eased forward on the slide and moved down it inch by slow inch, using his boots as a brake. Fen waited until he reached her side and his feet reached the soft-fall next to hers. She held out the apple juice, but he didn't take it.

'Want to tell me what those tears are for?'

Liam twisted the ear of a worn stuffed sheep and his mouth formed a pout. 'I don't want to live here.'

'Why not? We have lambs like the one you're holding. Real live ones. Down in the paddock near the river.'

'But I want to live where my mummy is.'

Fenella's heart skipped a beat. Had Kieran and Diane separated? 'Okay. And where is that, mate?'

Tears slid down his cheeks. 'She's an angel.'

~

Up at the cottage, Liv held out her hand and Kieran shook it. 'We have a deal.' He and Liam needed this. A clean break, a new start.

'It's going to be a challenge, Kieran. I can't promise you any different. Luke Sampson left this place in a mess and it's going to take some time to recover from it.' Her smile faded. 'Muzz will be turning in his grave knowing what that man did to us.'

Kieran shifted on his feet. He still couldn't believe Muzz was gone. A man larger than life with the patience of a saint and an infectious belly laugh. A man who could fix anything from heavy machinery to electronics, even teenage kids with attitude. 'I'm sorry, Liv. I'll do my best to turn it around for you.'

'I have complete faith in you. Fen blames herself for what happened. I've tried so hard to help her understand that it wasn't anyone's fault except that scoundrel Luke's.' Liv put her arm through his and they strolled back through the vines to the cellar door. 'Will Diane come over once you've settled in?'

And there it was, the question he'd known he wouldn't be able to avoid. The failure he preferred not to think about without a glass of something in his hand to make him forget. Kieran pushed open the gate leading into the gardens outside the cellar building. 'It's just Liam and I now. Diane passed away twelve months ago.'

'Oh, Kieran, I'm so sorry to hear that.' She squeezed his arm.

He let out a breath against the tightness in his chest. He'd never get over hearing those awful words that had echoed through the hospital corridors that day. *She's gone, mate, sorry. We did what we could to save her.*

'Thanks, Liv.'

The sound of crying reached his ears as they made their way into the play area. Kieran's heart tripped. He knew that cry well. He'd heard it so many times over the last twelve months. Had spent many a night holding back his own fears and doubts while he tried to still it. If only Liam hadn't been in the car with Diane that day then the nightmares that haunted his dreams, and sometimes his waking hours, wouldn't keep resurfacing. If only Kieran had paid closer attention to his wife.

'Oh dear,' Liv whispered. 'He sounds heartbroken.'

'Excuse me for a moment, Liv?'

'Of course, go to him.'

He hurried into the play area, fighting the ache in his chest that tried to slow his steps. Fen sat on the edge of the slide with Liam gathered in her lap, her arms around him, a glimmer of tears on her cheeks. He understood how she felt hearing those cries. Helpless, useless, powerless. Because he could never give Liam what his son needed most. His mother.

He knelt next to them and brushed a hand over his son's hair. 'Hey, mate. What's up?'

Liam stuck his thumb in his mouth and reached for Kieran with his other hand. As Fen's arms dropped away, he gathered his son to his chest and stood. Liam cuddled into him, his damp face buried against Kieran's neck.

'I'm so sorry. I had no idea,' Fen whispered.

He heard the regret in her voice and tried to keep the pain from his own. 'It's okay.' Except it wasn't. It might never be okay again. Not for Liam. 'It's been a long day for you, hasn't it, mate?' Kieran turned to Liv. 'Will it be alright if I swing by and sign the contract tomorrow?'

'Of course, love.'

'Thank you.' He turned back to Fen. 'Thank you for taking care of him. I appreciate it.'

'No problem.' She hugged her arms under her breasts, her eyes full of conflict and sadness.

He knew the thoughts that would be churning through her mind. He'd once been close enough to her to know her deepest, darkest secrets. Fen would be remembering what it was like to be abandoned, unwanted, unloved. To lose a mother the way he'd lost a father. To be adrift in a cold, hard world until they'd found peace and a home in the hearts of Wongan Creek.

Here, Liam could be with him out amongst the vineyards, away from the sad memories, and he'd have new people around him. As much as he owed the Vincents for giving him a chance in life, their grief at losing their daughter consumed them to the point where they no longer had a place in their hearts for Liam. Or him.

'Why don't you stay here tonight, Kieran?' Liv's suggestion fell into the silence that had settled awkwardly between them. 'Go into town and collect your things. Liam might feel better if he's settled sooner rather than later.'

No point delaying things further. It wasn't as if they had anything to keep them in town. All they'd brought with them from Sydney were clothes and toys. Everything else had been put into storage until he or the Vincents could deal with the sad memories and pain of parting with Diane's possessions.

'Are you sure?'

'Of course.' Liv patted his arm. 'We'll be ready for you when you come back. Take a couple of days to settle in. We have a wedding to cater for on Saturday, so we'll be busy all day. On Sunday we have breakfasts, lunches and tasting tours all booked. You can sit back and see what we do to get through the winter season before we put you to work on the clean-up in the vineyard.'

Fen stood and dusted off the seat of her denims. 'Will Liam be okay?'

The concern in her voice touched his heart. It had been a long time since Fen was a foster kid, but she'd understand the fears that went with strange places and people. 'He has a few favourite things he's brought over with him. I'll bring them over.'

'We'll make the transition as easy as possible for him.' She glanced at her watch. 'Okay, I'd better go and clean up. Those glasses won't wash themselves.' Fen brushed against him as she leaned over to pat Liam's back. 'See you later, mate. I'll save that Grumpy Lizard for when you come back.'

Liam's head moved under Kieran's chin as he looked at Fen and nodded. 'K.'

The single sound drifted out quietly from his son's lips and warmed some of the ice that gripped Kieran's soul. Liam was at least responding. It was more than he could ever have hoped for so soon. Perhaps in Fen his son had found a kindred spirit, a loner just like him.

Kieran tried to inject a lighter note into his voice he didn't feel and let a glimmer of hope warm him. Maybe coming home to Wongan Creek was a good idea after all. 'Right, we'll see you later then.'

Liv walked him out to the car and waited as he strapped Liam into his booster seat. Stepping back, he closed the door and looked out across the valley where rows and rows of vine leaves had turned brilliant shades of autumn colours. The quiet, peaceful view eased some of the tension from his shoulders. Across the creek, the Whispering Hills rose to meet the sky, as beautiful as he remembered them. He hadn't realised how much he'd missed them. So different from Sydney and the Blue Mountains, yet no less beautiful. If only Diane had loved Wongan Creek the way he did.

'It takes a while, love.' Liv's touch was soft on his sleeve. 'But time will heal the hurt and ease the loss.'

He shook his head slowly, hands on his hips as he watched an eagle soar over the ridge. If Liv only knew the full story … It would take more than time to heal, especially for Liam. But the less people knew about the way Diane died, the better. No matter what she'd done, he had to look after his son's interests first. Liam was his focus now.

'I hope so, Liv.' Because second chances and forgiveness were damn hard to earn.

Whispers, Secrets and Shadows (Wongan Creek Series) can be purchased from your favourite bookseller. If they don't have it, ask them or your local library to order it in for you.

Dear Reader

This book has been written and edited using Australian / UK English grammar and punctuation conventions because the story is set in Australia. For more information on the differences between UK and US language and punctuation, please consider reading this article: https://tinyurl.com/56tkbh6a

If you enjoyed this book, please consider leaving a review on BookBub, Goodreads or the platform you purchased it from. If you would prefer to email me, please visit the contact page on my website at https://juanitakees.com/contact/. I do love to hear from readers and welcome your feedback.

Kind regards

Juanita Kees

Other Books by Juanita Kees

Wongan Creek Series

Whispers

Secrets

Shadows

Unfinished Business

Exposed

Tagged

Silenced

Bindarra Creek

Home to Bindarra Creek

Promise Me Forever

The Calhouns of Montana

Montana Baby

Montana Daughter

Montana Son

Contemporary Romance

Finish Line

WINNER TAKES ALL
FINISH LINE
JUANITA KEES

9 781763 632400